The Hidden Faces of the Grand Canyon
A Galactic Ascent

by

Dominique Severina

A Novel

Dominique Severina Books are available for order
through Ingram Press Catalogues

This book is a work of fiction. Names, characters,
places and incidents either are products of the
author's imagination or are used fictitiously. Any
resemblance to actual persons, living or dead,
events or locales is entirely coincidental.
Dominique Severina
Visit my website at:
www. dominiqueseverina.com

Printed in the United States of America
First Printing: April 2016
Published by Sojourn Publishing, LLC

ISBN: 978-1-62747-196-1
Ebook ISBN: 978-1-62747-197-8

Table of Contents

Dedication

This book is dedicated to the oneness of the world we came here to share. May its seed still come to fruition.

To my mother, my father and my brother - all passed away - who taught me to see the infinitesimal as well as the vastness of the Universe.

Thank you for sharing your love of books and for teaching me to see and hear with my heart.

Acknowledgements

I wish to thank my husband for his love of the water, opening the world of rafting and the Grand Canyon to me. I am grateful also to all my family, friends and teachers. You know who you are and how precious you all are. You have helped me surf life and now the world of book writing and publishing. Your open heart and attentive ears have given me moments of joy and communion. Thank you for being on my path, and for having held out your hand for me. I cherish all of you. I appreciate you being in my life.

"We are not human beings having a spiritual experience. We are spiritual beings having a human experience."
—Pierre Teilhard de Chardin

Prologue

In this book, interwoven throughout the story, you will find historical and scientific information. I am providing some leads on how to research the different topics, if you so desire. I hope the story will trigger your curiosity to explore on your own – the Internet is making this really easy these days. Some of the literary sources can be taken more seriously than others.

This story invites you to become an active part of positive changes in the world.

To me it is important to listen to your heart and your intuition – and to find the truth within yourself.

Enjoy the ride,

Dominique Severina

"...Our deepest fear is not that we are inadequate.

Our deepest fear is that we are powerful beyond measure.

It is our light, not our darkness that most frightens us.

We ask ourselves, "Who am I to be brilliant, gorgeous, talented, fabulous?"

Actually, who are you not to be?

You are a child of God.

Your playing small does not serve the world.

There is nothing enlightened about shrinking so that other people won't feel insecure around you.

We are all meant to shine, as children do.

We were born to make manifest the glory of God that is within us.

It's not just in some of us; it's in everyone.

And as we let our own light shine, we unconsciously give other people permission to do the same.

As we are liberated from our own fear, our presence automatically liberates others."

This passage is commonly mis-attributed to Nelson Mandela's 1994 Inaugural Address.

It actually comes from the book, *A Return To Love,* by Marianne Williamson (1992).

"And now here is my secret, a very simple secret: It is only with the heart that one can see rightly; what is essential is invisible to the eye."
—Antoine de Saint-Exupéry

Chapter One

Return to the Future

Mia had just returned from an archeological conference. People had come from all over the galaxies to attend. It was the first one ever of such magnitude. The promised Golden Age had finally arrived, and peace had slowly settled into the hearts of all. After the First Contact on Earth, there had been a lot of turmoil. People didn't know what to believe or who to trust anymore. Over time, most of the humans had forgotten all their faculties, such as telepathy and listening to their hearts. Throughout the centuries, even the millennia, they had let a minority take over and control their daily lives.

With all the technology available, archeology had taken a huge turn. The full recovery of the twelve strands of human DNA – everyone's birthright – not only had helped to confirm theories from excavated material, but also allowed multidimensional travel back in time to relive precise, important moments. Not everybody was trained to do it, but Mia only needed to touch an artifact, and if she so desired, she could beam over into that time frame. She had done this many times before, but she realized she shouldn't attempt it during a full moon anymore because her emotions were too heightened then. The medical team, in fact, had confirmed an unusual overlap of lives during the last super moon. They weren't sure yet why this had happened, but Mia had a hunch. It occurred to her that perhaps she had been an archeologist in other lifetimes.

The more she delved into her research, the clearer it seemed that if she traveled to a time frame she knew she had previously lived in, she would lose her neutrality. She didn't want to mention it to the medical team, because they wouldn't allow her to study these specific periods of history. It seemed like a long time ago when she had come to a deep sense of knowing that history had to be rewritten. She promised herself to question what was accepted as truth, recognizing through her research that history all along had been manipulated to benefit only the few.

For Mia it was like living one life while awake, and living another while asleep. She was always very careful about going to sleep and waking up, making sure she knew which time frame she was living in. She was working hard not to get deeply involved in these other lifetimes. No one was more serious and professional than Mia. She knew the consequences – or so she thought.

"Use the raft to cross over the river," the Buddha advised, *"but don't carry it on your back for the rest of your life."*

Chapter Two

Creation Myths

Mia woke up from a deep sleep. What had she just said, or screamed? It felt as though she had tapped into time immemorial. Her whole body was shaking. She didn't know if this was out of fear, joy or some kind of anticipation. And then it dawned on her. It had all started with this little black-and-pink rock she'd found — or did it start eons ago?

She didn't even remember precisely where she had picked it up, somewhere deep inside the canyon. She just recalled that it looked like it was blinking at her, with its dusty rose eye in its center. "Take me with you," it seemed to say. Busy, getting ready to leave the river's shore, she put the rock in her pocket, even though she would have preferred to leave it *in situ*, exactly where she had found it. But this little stone — maybe one and a half times the size of her thumbnail — had a message for her from afar. And this message wouldn't manifest itself until more than two weeks after the trip down the Colorado River, through the Grand Canyon.

The river had left Mia enchanted, bewitched, and bemused. Something big had shifted for her. She felt that she was "in the secrets of the Gods," and had downloaded all the knowledge of the Earth, the universes, the galaxies and dimensions. Her cells were screaming, but she couldn't express that in words. It was like a lava flow, heating up and rising to inflame a deep-rooted passion for life, for knowing. There was a feeling of unity in diversity, of alpha and omega, of an all-encompassing sound that touched every cell in the animal, plant, mineral and human kingdoms.

At home, Mia soon fell back into her daily routine. She had emptied the pockets of her river shorts before washing them. In the Canyon, she and her friends had been told to tread lightly and pick up every bit of litter, right down to the micro trash they might find along the shores of the river and in their camping spots. She was now sifting through these potential treasures, and found the little rock again. "It could be Vishnu schist," she thought, a geological layer in the Grand Canyon that had fascinated her. Mia looked again at this perfectly shaped dusty rose circle in the middle of the small black rock. "Or," she wondered, "could it possibly be basalt with a rhyolite inclusion?"

As soon as she picked it up and held it in her hands, waves of memories came over her. Suddenly she was swimming among ocean waves, feeling like a dolphin being pushed to shore. The Dogon came to her mind, people living in West Africa guarding a cave with astonishing paintings. The dolphins are part of their creation myth.

She realized that the word she had been screaming in her previous dream – the one that had awakened her – was "Dogon." Then she remembered waking up from another dream many months ago, and saying the words, "Popol Vuh," three times. Both "Dogon" and "Popol Vuh," she recalled, are terms relating to creation myths.

Mia took a deep breath and thought, "What is my role? Who was I? Who am I? Why did I go on this river trip? I need to understand what is happening. I need to backtrack my lives."

"You are here to enable the divine purpose of the universe to unfold. That is how important you are."
—Eckhart Tolle

Chapter Three
Trip of a Lifetime

Years ago, Mia's husband Mickey told her that they had an invite to the Grand Canyon, but that they were on a waiting list for at least ten years. Everyone was talking about the rapids, especially the one called "Lava Falls." The years went by, and the more they talked about the river, the longer the rapids became and the bigger the waves grew in Mia's mind. She was not a water rat. Life and past life experiences had made her nervous about the element of water, but deep inside she knew, for her own sake, that she had to go. She decided to treat it as a vision quest. From that moment on, all her fears were gone. It now simply felt like a riddle. She could hear:

"That which you dream lies buried in the Canyon.

Enter with fearlessness at Lee's Ferry, an open space at the entrance of the Canyon.

The *'genius loci'* — the 'spirit of the place' — awaits, to take you down the river and lift the veil for you.

The rocks and the stones, the Keepers of the Earth and the Librarian of the Universe, are all ready to whisper their knowledge in your ear and enter your dreams.

Step through the dark to await the dawn.

The first ray of light is the most healing, bringing great blessings and knowledge from Divine Source.

Go and listen to the sounds."

And so Mia did. For eighteen days, she immersed herself in the energies and the spirit of the Grand Canyon. She could feel that there was something primordial in being there. It gave her a sense of deep reconnection. She had no earthly way to describe the beauty, the feelings and the emotions she encountered. Every word was used in a superlative, yet still, nothing was enough to express IT. Something happened to her at a cellular level.

Mia understood now that when she left the Grand Canyon, she definitely left a part of herself behind, or... had she found a part of herself that had always been there? She felt that she somehow had rediscovered her true, authentic self.

"Nevertheless, whether or not we care to admit it, human beings, like all living things, are part of a vast, intergalactic superorganism. Everything, from subatomic particles to single-cell organisms to the most distant stars in the galaxy, all are part of an indivisible Bond."
—Lynne McTaggart

Chapter Four

Memories of the Future

Mia was late for work. Her atomic watch had once again stopped in the middle of the night. Clocks never stopped on their own anymore. Cyber technology had solved that problem, but there was something mysterious going on around Mia. It took her weeks to comprehend what it was. On the days she traveled back in time – even unintentionally – to one of her past lives, the atomic clock would stop. The closest explanation was that she was leaving her galactic body to reenter a physical body, one she was familiar with from another lifetime. Deep within herself she thanked the clock for stopping; otherwise, there would have been no way for her to know about these unusual happenings. She only had hunches, until now. Mia would think about the technical aspect of it later. She got up and felt lightheaded. She instinctively knew that something big had happened during her sleep, "over there," as she often thought of it. She remembered a few glimpses, such as huge rock walls, a cave entrance, a running river – and a feeling of urgency.

But she couldn't respond to these feelings now — she had to get going.

Today the archeological lab was expecting a visit from a highly advanced scientist who was involved in an enormous number of key excavations — excavations Mia could only dream of.

One part of her was excited; the other was exhausted. "Come on," she told herself, "get a grip." She went to the kitchen, which was a mixture of high technology and late nineteenth-century "Grandmother's Kitchen" style with shiny copper pans. The ship's decorator had done a great job, understanding her yearning for antique-looking appliances adapted to the advanced technology on a spaceship. Her friends laughed whenever they visited, and suggested she could have at least chosen the mid-twentieth century, but there was a coziness about her kitchen that attracted a lot of her friends. They all had food replicators, and none of them were doing any cooking at all anymore. Mia had also continued the habit of making her own coffee. She had her connections. She not only used an old French press and an Italian espresso machine, she was still cooking on the stove. Though the stove looked like an elephant from a past century, nobody criticized her coffee — it was the best in this galaxy. Mia was thankful that none of her friends had paid her a surprise visit this morning.

As she thought back, she realized that whenever she had time traveled to one of her past lives, she would sense an unspoken, strong protection, like being in a cocoon. It appeared to her that something was making her return to the past to figure out an enigma, or many of them; to find a clue, or even something that might have belonged to her. "Enough of this for now," she thought.

The divine smell of coffee, and her homemade breakfast of eggs, green chili and goat cheese wrapped in a fresh tortilla, sent her straight back into her galactic body. Again, she was thankful for all the good connections she had when it came to food. Nothing could replace quality food, not even a replicator.

Mia put one of her lighter jumpsuits on, which was both sporty and elegant, accentuating her perfectly shaped, svelte body. She brushed her short black hair and rushed to the lab down the hallway. For the past eight years, she had been living on this huge mothership. She had chosen the spaceship over the space station because it was designed for far-reaching exploration of the galaxies. It was always on the move. It had allowed her to be at the forefront of the research, and still decorate her private quarters in an antique style, as her friends liked to remark. She needed this balance — it was comforting to her.

Her dream was to eventually move to the New Earth – "Terra Christa" – but her knowledge and gifts were highly valued, and needed, in the scientific as well as the spiritual world.

"Our great human adventure is the evolution of consciousness. We are in this life to enlarge the soul and light up the brain."
—*Tom Robbins*

Chapter Five

Crossing Paths

The scientist was already at the lab. He was studying Mia's library and didn't hear her come in. She was one of a few on the spaceship who still had bookcases – adapted to the environment of a spaceship – and full of real books. Everyone else was using their highly sophisticated computers. Mia came from a family who always had books, and she had inherited a whole collection from her grandfather, who was an avid archeologist in his own right. She had some rare editions of illuminated manuscripts going back to the Middle Ages. They were her pride and joy.

Startled by her presence, the scientist quickly turned around. Their eyes met and locked for quite a while. A wave of memories seemed to overcome each of them. He finally broke the silence. "Mia, I presume?" His tone of voice didn't correspond to the feelings they were sharing. Mia straightened her collar that she always preferred to keep up. She hadn't looked up his file and didn't know his first name. Everyone called him "Bonehead" – a nickname he was unaware of, hopefully. It wasn't disrespectful, but more of a compliment. He could name every single bone of the human body and of every other species. This time, with a warm, deep voice and a handshake, he said, "My name is Michael." When their hands touched, another wave engulfed them. They both quickly retracted their hands and put them in their pockets. An awkward moment passed, then they laughed.

"I heard that you have unique abilities and technologies to travel through time," he said. She kind of giggled, not knowing where this was leading. As far as she knew, he was primarily a scientist. "Let's cut to the chase," he continued. "I've heard a lot about you. You seem to have a gift. We both know that science is not obsolete. And the addition of ten more DNA[1] strands has given us – as we both know – a palette of new possibilities, such as supporting a multidimensional consciousness that was always meant to be our natural state. But currently, you seem to be the only person who — without using any type of device — can literally evaporate from this spaceship and reappear in another lifetime as if there was nothing to it. I would like to invite you to become a part of my team, and observe you closely. There also are certain times in the past that I would like to send you back to. I am not convinced that we have figured out how to choose where to go. It seems that you get sent to certain places, whether you want to or not. I am sure you would appreciate being able to control it better."

"You mean you want me to be a guinea pig?" Mia asked, in an irritated tone. Whatever was happening to her was a very private matter, she felt. She didn't want to be poked, examined, observed and followed. On the other hand, she felt somehow that she was holding a key to a vast endeavor. She needed someone she could trust, especially during the uneasy moments when she disappeared and then materialized in another lifetime. Yes, everyone knew how to beam over – but her encounters were of a different nature.

Even though she had just met Michael, something about him made her feel safe. In the work they were both doing, it was important to have a good crew one could count on. Until now, Mia had been a lone wolf in her department. The field of archeology had broadened so much over the last century that it not only involved studying the past, but now also included exploring new worlds, lives and civilizations. The "Trekkies" would say "go where no man has gone before."[2] Everyone on the mothership had watched the old "Star Trek" TV series and films by Gene Roddenberry. Some had even created a "Star Trek" club. They were all fascinated to see how people on Earth viewed life in space.

"I'll tell you what," Michael said. "Why don't you just join the team under the pretext that we need to combine forces, and our knowledge, so that we may optimize archeological science? From now on, let's do an occasional expedition together. Viewed from the outside, it will look like an effort to advance both the science and our teamwork. The rest will be just between you and me, until we figure out what is happening to you. I have to admit that I might be experiencing something similar. I haven't talked about it because it makes me feel vulnerable, and it is not a subject I want to discuss with just anyone. For whatever reason, it only took me a fraction of a second, when I first saw you, to know that you were the person I could share this with. So, what do you think?"

While Michael was talking, Mia could see this unique glow of light, shining mist or shimmering dust surrounding him. For as long as she could remember, she would see it appear around people she could trust. The mist was merging with hers, although she wasn't doing anything physically to make that happen. "Okey-dokey," she said lightly. Whenever she had to make a big decision, her choice of words seemed a bit off, as if she didn't want to acknowledge the importance of the commitment. This way it was somehow taking the edge off the seriousness of her decision. Michael raised his eyebrow in question, but the energy he could feel from Mia confirmed that they had just sealed a pact for life.

"...the separation between past, present, and future is only an illusion, although a convincing one."
—*Albert Einstein*

Chapter Six

Cellular Memories

Mia was standing in her lab, looking at a map of Earth. It was definitively a place that seemed to inspire her. Her parents and grandparents — all her ancestors – had come from there.

She remembered, as a child, repeatedly staring at a picture hanging above her dad's desk. It was dated December 24th, 1968. It depicted the "Earthrise" that greeted the Apollo 8 astronauts as they emerged from behind the Moon.[3] She still could hear her father's deep voice telling her, "From space, Earth appeared blue because of the waters of the oceans that covered more than seventy percent of the planet." There was sadness in his voice. At the time when the picture was taken, Earth was the only known planet in our solar system that had enough water to support natural life.

Mia was born on a space station, because by then her grandparents were trying to escape the rapidly declining environmental and political living conditions on Earth. For years, they worked in the archeological field all over the world. Having a pretty good understanding of why some civilizations faded away, they were hired to work on a space program, focused on finding another inhabitable planet with similarities to Earth when it still was pristine. The water situation had become very precarious, and the drought had turned many areas into deserts. For most of its inhabitants, Earth wasn't viable anymore.

Both sets of grandparents had only one child. The two of them, a girl and a boy, grew up like siblings, with their parents working together and always living close to each other. They didn't want their only children to battle for survival, so at a young age they sent them to live on a space station. They were both fourteen years old when they started their training at the Space Fleet Academy. As a final exam, each got appointed to do research in a different area of a little-known galaxy. This separation made them realize that they were in love with each other. Soon afterward they married, and eventually Mia was born. None of them ever returned to Earth.

Mia was still a young child when her parents were killed in a freak accident. Their space cruiser crashed onto an uninhabitable planet, due to a technical defect. The shock and loss had been immeasurable for Mia. She had been very close to and fond of her parents, and after they died, she didn't speak for three months. All of her grandparents moved permanently to the space station to raise her. That is how she got her passion for archeology.

Mia snapped out of her daydream, and concentrated again on the map in front of her. She focused her gaze on North America. For her birthday, a friend had given her a book on the Grand Canyon. She remembered reading that it was called one of the seven natural wonders of the world. The book contained some detailed maps of the Canyon. Someone had left notes, postcards and newspaper clippings in it, and even a few pages of a diary, written in longhand, describing the Canyon. At the bottom of the last page was the letter M. It looked as though the book had been used a lot, and had lived through many adventures.

As she read the names of the places in the Canyon, she felt something very familiar about it. It was love, yearning, fear, astonishment – and a feeling of being lost and found again.

She hadn't been able to fall asleep that night. Her discussion with Michael had left her pensive. Everything moved so fast, and at the same time felt so profound. Even though she had just met him, here they were, already sharing secrets like little children. "This is a good sign," she thought. "Children instinctively know who and what to trust." For many years, Mia had studied books written in the first half of the twentieth century by an educator named Maria Montessori.[4] It felt as though they were written for today's world – so appropriate, and so advanced for their day – but also timeless. Montessori had really distilled the educational process down to its essence. Mia always thought that knowing about education would also help her find clues in the archeological field. In a sense, archeology was digging in the soil – and good education was digging in the soul.

Tonight was a full moon. Even though she couldn't see it from the location of the mothership, she could feel its energy, since all her ancestors had come from planet Earth.

Humans had always been very sensitive to the moon's energies.

Mia remembered what the medical team had said: "Don't time travel on these special days." She knew that she'd only time traveled to one location during the full moon — the Grand Canyon. But she realized that the different lifetimes in which she had lived, or visited it, had overlapped. Why this confusion? She had to figure it out. It really gave her an edgy feeling. Once again, she could feel and hear:

"Deep in the Canyon, past, present and future are one. Time is just a memory. With this comes the feeling of oneness with the Universe, and with the galaxies – and the lifting of the veil between the dimensions."

Mia knew that each universe, galaxy, planet, star – each soul – had a divine plan. Now she deeply sensed that she not only had to work on her own divine plan, but also on the one of her soul group, her planet, her galaxy and dimension. She suddenly felt on a cellular level how important and unique every single person is. She was reminded of her favorite teachings. These always seemed to invite her to start out there in the galaxies, and slowly zoom in to Earth – its different continents, its countries, its diversities.

Mia turned her attention back to the map in the book. The different names of the canyons, rims and ridges caught her eye. As she turned the book to a different angle to read the names better, a newspaper clipping fell out and sailed under the desk. "I'll get it later," she thought. Then she leaned over the map again, and looked at the names along the river. Her gaze stopped around the area between Trinity Creek and Ninety-four Mile Creek, on the north side of the Colorado River. "What are all these Egyptian names?" Mia wondered. Slowly she read them aloud: "Isis Temple, Osiris Temple, Tower of Set, Tower of Ra, Tower of Horus, Cheops Pyramid." Mia started to sweat. Her breath became shallow. She was feeling sick to her stomach. An indescribable dizziness came over her, and she felt lightheaded. Slowly she hunched over and tried to prop herself on the desk, but her hands only grabbed emptiness. She hit her head on the corner of the desk – and everything went black.

"If you talk to a man in a language he understands, that goes to his head. If you talk to him in his language, that goes to his heart."
—Nelson Mandela

Chapter Seven

Back in Time

Mia was enjoying her Grand Canyon trip down the Colorado River. After going downriver for fifty miles, she felt she had finally found her "river legs." In the rapids, she was holding on and going with the flow – "high-siding," if necessary. The waves were pretty big, and most of the time they covered the whole raft, but she trusted her husband Mickey. He was a good oarsman, and they wouldn't flip. The water was cold. Flowing through Glen Canyon Dam, it originated from the bottom of the Lake Powell reservoir, where no sun rays ever hit. By the time the water entered the Grand Canyon, it was around fifty degrees. With the hot sun, though, wearing shorts and a tank top was comfortable at this time of the year, as summer temperatures in the Canyon often exceed 100 degrees Fahrenheit.

The narrow gorge held the heat in its bosom deep into the night, sometimes keeping the tired crew awake. The early morning hours would be a welcome relief.

Feeling more comfortable around the element of water now, Mia began tapping deeper into the energies of the Canyon. She always had been very empathic. Over the last two days, she had experienced some strange sensations. They had stopped at Redwall Cavern, a vast chamber carved by the river over time. Mia felt at home instantly, and she shook her sandals off her feet. She could see and feel each toe being slowly engulfed in the cool sand. It felt as if every grain of sand had a story to tell. As she toned wordlessly, she started to dance to the sounds of a drum and guitar that her friends were playing. Soon she fell into a trance – and she suddenly was a Native American woman. Her life story lay before her eyes. She saw herself, and her two little children, inching down a steep path on the North Rim of the Grand Canyon toward the river. Pregnant again, she was running away from an abusive relationship. She was familiar with the Canyon since her early childhood, and knew every detail of the area. She had spent wonderful moments in its womb, learning to fish, hunt and gather edible mushrooms and medicinal plants. She was known for her healing abilities.

The woman was planning to check on the granaries in the cliffside that her people, the Anasazi, had built. She knew that she and her children would be able to survive, and have a good life, in the shadow of the Canyon, respecting Mother Nature's rhythms.

Mia was lightheaded and stopped dancing. She felt hot, and suddenly so tired. She wasn't sure where she had just gone. Feeling drawn to touch her hair, she was astonished to find how short it was, since she could still feel the weight of long, straight, black hair. She looked down to see that she was wearing river shorts, but the skin of her legs remembered the touch of soft leather. She put her hands on her flat belly and felt as if something was missing. She shook her head and looked around. Her friends had stopped playing their instruments and were resting in the cavern's shade. Mia just dropped to the sand where she was standing, and fell fast asleep.

"Forgiveness is the fragrance that the violet sheds on the heel that has crushed it."
—*Mark Twain*

Chapter Eight

The Dream of the Cave

The sun was beating down on the path. There was no breeze whatsoever. After hours of a grueling, steep descent, then an ascent, the group of archeologists and scientific researchers finally reached the entrance of the cave. It was more of a mountaineering endeavor than a Sunday outing. Luckily, they found a flat spot for their tent further down in a little side canyon, away from the main trail. They were careful not to pitch it right below the cave entrance. Rockslides were highly probable, dangerous, and frequent in this area of the Canyon. Previous rainfalls had loosened many rocks and made it hazardous.

It had taken weeks to organize this expedition. Researchers from all over the world were invited to join. After long deliberations, the museum's administration had agreed to allow the renowned archeologist's daughter to join the group. Its members did not feel that this was the place for a woman, but her father Paul had insisted. He argued that he could not have a better assistant than his own daughter. Mimi had accompanied him on every single excavation since his wife had passed away three years ago. She was glad she had been in desert-like countries before, because she knew how to protect herself from the sun. Other than her father, the rest of the group looked as if they had just left the office. Some of them still had on suits, ties and inadequate shoes. "It must be due to working inside a museum," she thought, shaking her head in disbelief.

The director of the museum wanted to join the expedition as well. He was convinced that they were looking for the find of the century, and that it would change the history of the world. According to the story, and the report by the geologist who had discovered the cave, it must have been inhabited by an "Oriental" race, or possibly Egyptian. "How could this even be possible?" he wondered. He had to see it with his own eyes, yet he hadn't participated in an excavation for more than twenty years. He had enough to deal with in the museum itself. Today he was just thinking that being in a cool stone building had some advantage. Originally they wanted to wait for a better season, but everyone was eager to work on this project.

At camp they had split into small groups. The museum's director wanted to explore the cave first. One group accompanied him to the entrance and evaluated the situation. The geologist had already shown him lots of plans and drawings of his findings. A long main passage led to a big room on the left, in which they found mummies. Following this passage further into the cave, a multitude of other pathways radiated like spokes of a wheel into several chambers. Most of the cave had been carved out of the rock by human hand. The find consisted of a vast array of pottery, idols, and various tools made of copper, as well as urns with hieroglyphs on them. The geologist speculated that thousands of people could have been living in this cave.

Mimi wanted to stay back and take a few notes in her diary. It had always helped her dad later on when she showed him written observations she had made during their expeditions. She had a unique way of seeing things. Besides, she needed some space. The group of men was not used to having a female presence on an archeological dig. She was thinking of how proud she had been earlier in the year, when the first International Women's Day was observed in the United States on February 28th, 1909.[5] It would still take years before women in America would have the right to vote. She took a deep breath. Archeology was still a man's world.

Three hours later, the small group returned – exhausted from the heat and the steep climb, but exhilarated about the discovery.

As the lead archeologist, her father gathered everyone and gave each of them an assignment for the next day. They needed a precise topography of the cave and all its archeological findings. The artifacts and the layout of the mummies in their tombs had to be documented thoroughly. Another group would go deeper into the cave to see if there was more to be discovered.

They all had dinner and went to bed early. The days were already getting very hot, so the earlier they got up, the better.

The moon was disappearing in the early morning light. During the night, Mimi heard two other people arriving. "The full moon must have lit their way," she thought, pulling the cover over her shoulders, suddenly chilled. The previous afternoon, she had helped put up an additional tent, expecting the late arrival of the rest of the crew. It appeared that these two geologists had already left for the cave before dawn.

Everyone was finishing breakfast and getting ready to hike to the cave again. This time Mimi would come along to the entrance and take more notes.

The climb was steep. She decided to walk up to the cave last so that she could take her time and enjoy the views. But her hopes were dashed when she saw one of the scientists, Bob, having a hard time walking. His shoes were inadequate for such a rugged trail. As the rocks started to slide under his feet, he suddenly lost his balance, fell, and rolled down past Mimi. A big boulder on the path stopped his fall.

"Thank goodness," she thought. Nevertheless, his landing was hard. His facial expression wasn't promising. "Are you okay?" Mimi asked.

He seemed to be in pain and replied, "I think I just twisted my ankle."

"Can you still walk?" she inquired.

"If I don't take my boot off, I should at least be able to make it back to camp, with your help," he sighed.

Above them, two other members of the group had witnessed the incident. As they called out, "Do you need help?" an echo amplified their voices. Together Mimi and Bob replied, "No, thank you, we will manage." They started walking back to the camp, slowly and carefully, with Bob using Mimi's shoulder as a support.

Meanwhile, Mimi's father had already entered the cave with a smaller group. They were planning to go further inside. In the chamber with all the mummies, he felt elated like everyone else, but the deeper they ventured into the cave, the more uncomfortable he became. He had always been very sensitive to his surroundings, and to changing energies. He stopped and turned around to face the group that was following him. "We need to go slowly. We are dealing with some kind of energy here that is unfamiliar to me," he said. "With every step, I am feeling a shift in the energy – as if something won't let me go further. An invisible force is pushing me back."

Even though the museum's director had felt a certain resistance too, he insisted: "I didn't come this far only to give up on a whim. We have to go to the end of the cave, if there even is one. I chose my men, and we will check it out – with or without you."

Paul could feel a sudden animosity coming from the group. He started to lose his patience. Until now, his expertise had always been respected and trusted. He gathered himself and said, "With all due respect, I am heading out. I am following my gut feelings, and I highly recommend that you join me. We need to take this one step at a time. We are encountering some advanced knowledge and technologies here, believe it or not. There are certain things about the past that we still don't have explanations for – and you know the stories about curses when excavating tombs in Egypt. There is always some truth to a legend. I am heading back to the entrance to study the material there, for a while. It might give us some more clues." His speech didn't have any effect on the rest of the crew. The attraction of this treasure was too great. And nobody really wanted to go back to the midday heat of the Canyon. Paul stuck to his guns, and stormed back to the entrance by himself to think things through and continue exploring. He wondered where Mimi was.

Slowly helping Bob down the steep path, Mimi discovered a little side canyon. After asking him to take a break and sit down for a minute, she quickly explored the walls of the canyon. In a little alcove, she found a deep enough fissure to slide her backpack, with her diary inside, to hide it from indiscreet eyes. She wanted to be able to support Bob down the trail without being hindered by a pack. They continued their arduous descent. Suddenly they heard footsteps behind them. They both turned their heads around. It was her father, who looked upset. His facial expression showed concern when he saw Mimi supporting Bob. Without a word, he grabbed Bob's arm, and together they found their way back to camp.

"What is going on?" Mimi asked her dad. He remarked that there were different energies emanating from the back of the cave — ones he had never felt before — as if somebody were trying to keep them from going any further. For him, every archeological site had a type of energy to deal with — whether from the site itself, its geological components, or its location – or due to events that had happened there in the past. All of these factors could easily have an influence here. Some places were cursed. This one not only felt cursed, but there was a sense of danger and unwelcoming to it. He knew of places that were protected by some kind of energy field. To him, this was one of them.

Before they left for the expedition, Paul had held a meeting about those types of risks. He reminded everyone about what had happened in some pyramids when closed-off chambers were opened. "That won't happen to us," everyone said. "Be a scientist, not an intuitive," one of them remarked, while sharing a drink afterward. This had infuriated Paul, but he simply couldn't convince anybody.

"I did what I had to do. That is all I can do," he thought, frustrated. Now they were in the Canyon, and still nobody would listen to his concerns. This time they were really justified.

At camp, Paul and Mimi helped Bob remove his boot. His ankle was now rapidly swelling. Mimi had a good healing salve in her personal medicine bag. On her travels she had met a healer, a wise woman who had shared some of her healing salves and tonic recipes and taught her some healing techniques.

Knowing that this would help Bob, Mimi applied the salve, bandaged his foot and ordered him to rest. She then prepared a small meal for the three of them.

After lunch, her father talked again about the strange energy he felt in the cave. "At one point, I thought I was hallucinating. Far in the back I could see a glow. I mentioned it to the others, but they just laughed. Also, there seem to be a huge number of Egyptian-looking artifacts, but I was not getting the same energy signature from them that I felt when we were in Egypt."

Mimi nodded and said, "I know what you mean. I couldn't put my finger on it either, but you are right, it is not just Egyptian." She continued, "Dad, did I ever tell you that Frank let me choose my wedding ring? That's so unusual." She took a deep breath, and her eyes got moist. Two years ago, after they had been married for only a short time, her husband had died while on an archeological dig in Egypt. The walls of a tomb had crumbled down, killing him instantly. "I still try not to think about it, but I can't help it. It feels like it happened yesterday, mainly because of our findings here, in this cave."

"No, actually, I don't think you told me the story," her dad invited her to continue, touched that for the first time since the tragedy, Mimi was finally sharing her feelings. Frank was still a very painful subject between them, and Paul tried to avoid it. Time would help with the healing process.

Mimi followed her train of thought. "When we went to the goldsmith, we asked for wedding bands. He suggested to Frank that he let me choose something more special, saying that this was a once-in-a lifetime thing to do. Frank agreed, which I didn't expect. I hadn't thought about having a ring other than a simple gold band, but I knew that I liked lapis lazuli. I looked at the jeweler's bookshelf and pulled out a catalogue on Egyptian art. Browsing through it, I saw a ring that I instantly fell in love with. It had a lapis scarab and a motif of palm leaves on the sides. "That is what I want," I said. It looked like it was meant for me. Then, the night before our wedding, I had a dream that in a past life I had a bracelet like that, but that in this lifetime I was only going to have the ring. When I woke up, I was curious. Sometime after the wedding, we paid a visit to the goldsmith. I grabbed the book where I had seen the picture of the ring. Below it was a caption I hadn't read before — Egyptian Woman's Bracelet. With certainty, I knew that this bracelet had belonged to me a long time ago, and that in this lifetime, I was meant to have the ring."

Paul was watching the change in his daughter's facial expression as she told the story. Her features became finer and more regal, as if an overlap of personalities was occurring. Her skin started to glow. He just watched, not commenting on it. Then he said, "What a marvelous story that is, Mimi. Once more it proves that we are part of something much bigger. Also, you were always attracted to the Egyptian culture. You accompanied your mother and me on excavations in Egypt when you were very little, and here we are now, in the Grand Canyon, excavating artifacts that are possibly Egyptian. This is something that I need to wrap my mind around. It doesn't seem logical to me." He waited a moment, then said, "I am glad you shared this with me. It brings us even closer together. You remind me a lot of your mother, Mimi. She never got enough of Egypt, even when she was pregnant with you and accompanied me to that hot, but beautiful, unique country. Before she died, she handed me a necklace. She told me to give it to you when you turned twenty-five years old – and that is only two months from now." He was shaking his head in disbelief at how fast the time had flown.

"Oh, dad," Mimi said, "I miss her so much. I still don't understand why she got so sick from the water and we didn't. Her system must have been weaker than ours. I can feel her everywhere, in every rock, every flower. How lucky we are to have spent all that time together." Her dad moved closer to her. "I am so glad that you, too, have the archeological bug. I know it has brought happiness, but also hardship, to our family." For a moment they both drifted into their own worlds.

After a while, they checked on Bob, who was fast asleep, recovering from his fall. "Let me meditate on the situation here, and find a proper way to safely do our archeological research," Paul commented. "Talking about Frank suddenly brought back the feeling that he might have died because of a curse on his archeological dig," he added, shaking his head. They both took a deep breath. "I am going to take a nap," he continued. "Sometimes it helps me find solutions." He hugged Mimi the way he did when she was little, then he lay down under a bush that barely provided enough shade to cover his tall body.

Mimi wanted to write in her diary, but remembered that she had hidden her backpack with the diary inside in the protected alcove. "Why did I do that?" she thought. "It is like leaving a good friend behind. I guess I will take a nap too, and then go back up when the sun fades from this wall." She lay down, ready to fall into the arms of Morpheus.

"Don't give up, just be you, because this life is too short to be anybody else."
—Unknown

Chapter Nine

Where the Times Meet

Michael had just come back from a short archeological excavation. His crew had been very helpful — they all were scientists. He appreciated the thoroughness of their work, but for right now he needed somebody with more intuition and transcendental abilities. He couldn't get Mia out of his mind. He'd never had such strong feelings for a person he'd just met. There was a sensation of well-being, comfort, and understanding without a need for words, which totally threw him off. "I have to go see her, he thought, "under the pretense of checking out a book from her grandfather's library." He also wanted to run a few details of today's excavation by her. And a day on the mothership would be good for a change. Cruising across the galaxies was fabulous, but sometimes his gypsy life weighed heavily on his shoulders.

Michael had given his crew two days off, and he had left with his little "puddle jumper" shuttlecraft. After docking it onto the mothership, he went down the hallway toward the lab, where he had first met Mia the day before. It was getting late, but he knew that it was likely he'd find researchers still at work. He could see some light shimmering through the curtains. "Who else is still using curtains? Nobody. Funny," he thought. He felt like barging into the lab, as if they had known each other for years, but he changed his mind.

Michael didn't have to search too long for a door ringer. A big, antique cowbell was hanging there, waiting to be rung. As soon as he touched it, a deep gong emanated from it. Michael listened to the sound, carried away by the waves. Nobody answered, so he finally opened the door. Light music was playing inside. There was a strong smell of coffee in the air. "Perfect, this is just what I need; a cookie would be good, too," he mused.

"Mia, are you here?" he called out. "It's me, Michael." She didn't answer. He walked to the bookcase, slid the airtight door open and grabbed the book he had wanted to check out, about the Grand Canyon on planet Earth. He'd always had a fascination for the area. It triggered something inside him, but he hadn't been able to pinpoint the cause yet. "Maybe Mia could help," he thought. Putting the book on the lab table, he wandered around. He suddenly felt a weird energy. Out of the blue, he started to become concerned about Mia. "What is going on with me, from tough guy to being worried about a colleague I just met yesterday?" He was shaking his head, not in denial, but more in wonder. "Where did she go?" He suddenly heard a sweeping noise and kind of a moan. He followed the sound. The back part of the office, with the desk, was barely lit. He could see a dark form moving. He instantly knew something was wrong.

"Mia!" He clapped his hands, and that part of the room lit up. Mia was lying halfway under the desk. There was dried blood on the floor. He knelt down, as Mia started coming back to her senses. He helped her try to sit up. "Slowly," he said. "You have quite a bump and a cut on your head. What happened?" She looked at him with her big, questioning eyes. He felt relieved. Her pupils were normal; no head trauma. He still wanted to grab a laser and check her out to make sure that nothing was broken. The first aid kit had all the necessary tools. Medical treatment had evolved greatly. There were a lot of new technologies that facilitated a diagnosis, and going to the doctor was now mostly a thing of the past. They were still around, but mainly for life-threatening ailments, which barely existed anymore. The galactic body was able to regenerate itself in no time.

Michael helped Mia get up and sit comfortably. He brought her a glass of water, then retrieved the laser from the first aid kit. "You are already healing your wound, but it will feel good to laser the spot." As soon as he directed the laser, the lesion disappeared. "How are you feeling?" he asked, relieved to see her cheeks getting rosy again.

"Better, thank you," Mia said. "I don't know what happened. I was studying a map of the Grand Canyon, when I suddenly felt dizzy and fell. Everything went black for a moment. Then it felt as if I were splitting in two. My galactic body must have stayed here. I slipped into what we call a physical body, and traveled back to the twentieth century."

She shivered at the thought. She remembered feeling wet and cold, but somehow satisfied and happy. Then again, she felt worried and oppressed. "I think I know where I was. I was on a rafting trip, going down the Colorado River in the Grand Canyon. I also must have been climbing up a very steep cliff."

"Wait a minute," Michael said. "Did you really say "Grand Canyon," as in THE Grand Canyon on planet Earth?" His eyes were wide with astonishment.

"Yes," Mia answered. "My great-grandfather was a geologist in the United States. He spent half his life exploring and writing about it." Michael's face lit up, as he said, "Oh, this is the book I saw the other day, and I came back today to look at it closely, with your permission, of course. My great-grandfather also had a love for this Canyon, and I have the feeling that many keys to understanding the Universe are hidden in its rocks."

"I think I can stand up now," Mia said. "Oh, of course," Michael replied. "I was caught up in thoughts of the Grand Canyon." He gently pulled her to her feet. She seemed okay. "Oh, wait," she said. "There is a newspaper clipping under the desk that fell out of the book I was looking at. We can put it back where it belongs. The book is bursting at the seams with all the added material inside." Michael ducked under the desk. Mia's fall had pushed the article further underneath it. It was pretty dark, so he had to squint his eyes. Michael couldn't wait to peek at it. The title was written a little bigger than the rest of the article. He read something like "Explora...." The ink had faded over time. Then something like "Gr... Canyon." Michael had forgotten where he was. "Grand Canyon again!" he screamed, hitting his head on the underside of the desk. His scream turned into a moan, accompanied by Mia's exclamation of "Oh, no," and her giggling. "We are quite a pair of scientists. Aren't we?! Come out from down under, and let me laser your bump."

Grumbling, Michael stood back up and replied, "Funny you should say that. My grandfather told me that as a child, he loved to hide under his grandpa's desk, hoping he wouldn't know. His grandpa would ignore his presence for a while and then suddenly acknowledge him. It would scare my grandfather, and he would hit his head on the desk. "Come out from down under," his grandpa would say. Of course, there were no lasers then. He would send his grandson to his grandmother to put some arnica salve on his bump. All of those bumps my grandfather got must have made me super-intelligent," he said.

"That still has to be proven," Mia commented laughingly. Then she turned serious again. "Let's look at this article."

"The glories and the beauties of form, color, and sound unite in the Grand Canyon – forms unrivaled even by the mountains, colors that vie with sunsets, and sounds that span the diapason from tempest to tinkling raindrop, from cataract to bubbling fountain."
—John Wesley Powell

Chapter Ten

The Lost Continent

In the bright light of the lab, Mia and Michael could now make out the whole title of the front-page article: "Explorations in Grand Canyon: Remarkable Finds Indicate Ancient Egyptian People Migrated from the Orient." It appeared in the Phoenix, Arizona "Gazette" on April 5th, 1909, and described a potential underground city in the Grand Canyon.[6] The discovery was made by an explorer named G.E. Kinkaid, who found a large cave with multiple passages and rooms carved by humans. There he discovered tablets with hieroglyphs, bronze tools, different statues with Egyptian and Tibetan features, a statue of

Buddha, and mummies. The long article mentioned an expedition financed by the Smithsonian Institution.

"It is curious," Mia said. "Just reading this part of the article, it feels so familiar to me, as if I were just there. I must have been. I can still sense, in and around my body, partial memories of where I went and what I did. Before I fell, I did not have these sensations, at least not this strong. The overlapping of lifetimes in my "out-of-galactic-body experiences" has been more intense than ever, and it looks like it will get even more so. Please help me figure this out."

Michael replied, "I will, and I agree with you. I also have to tell you that ever since I can remember, I know there is something I have to figure out about the Grand Canyon myself. It seems that my great-grandfather took something, some knowledge with him to his grave, and I need to find out what it is. My own grandfather doesn't know it either. The first step is to find out how we can travel back to the precise time and place where we want to go. There is something of great importance to be found there."

Mia responded, "Let's call it quits for tonight. We've had more than our fill of excitement for one day. And since we've both hit our heads, we should get some rest now. There are some fabulous rejuvenation chambers here on the mothership – and good old-fashioned beds. I personally need a good night's sleep in my own bed. What about you?"

"A bed sounds divine. Is the 'All-Fashion Inn' still open?" Michael asked.

"Oh, yes," she answered, "but it is always booked. You may crash at my place. It's something like a condo, with two adjacent living quarters. One is vacant right now, so you are welcome to use it. It has a lovely antique bed, with a thick mattress and wonderful linen sheets. Nothing can replace the feeling of a comfy bed."

"Thank you, I accept. The past few weeks have been short on sleep. Also, we will be able to think better after some well-earned rest," Michael mumbled, then yawned deeply.

From the lab, they walked down the hall of the mothership to Mia's condo. Michael knew right away which one was hers — beside the doors hung a range of different-sized antique cowbells. They entered without ringing them.

Mia showed Michael to his quarters, bidding him good night, then headed to hers. A hot shower and her fluffy bed were all she needed. When her head hit the pillow she suddenly felt as if she were on a flying carpet, taking her away. With a shiver, she pulled the blankets tighter around herself.

*"Above all else, guard your heart, for
everything you do flows from it."*
—Proverbs 4:23

Chapter Eleven

Message from the Canyon

A cold wind was blowing over the edge of
the Canyon. The sky had snowy white hues. "I
am glad you came back," Mia heard whispered
in her ear. She looked around, but didn't see
anybody who wasn't part of the group. The
voice sounded kind of otherworldly. It was less
the sound than the feeling she had — like a
message from afar.

Around her, the rafts were being filled up
with air. They had to get rigged before dark.
The majority of the group of sixteen people
had come in later than planned, because they
had been caught in a snowstorm near
Flagstaff. The visibility was bad, and it felt like
being in a cocoon. When they finally arrived at
Lee's Ferry, it was already afternoon. They
started to unload the trucks and trailers.
Though most of the people knew each other, it

was a weird feeling to know they would all share eighteen days of their lives together, to raft down the Colorado River in the Grand Canyon.

Mia saw the park ranger arrive in her white truck. As she stepped out of the vehicle, a good-looking man seemingly appeared, behind her, out of nowhere. Mia noted his presence. He had a very regal appearance, with an aquiline nose, and a steady, profound energy.

At some point, Mia's attention returned to the ranger. The whole crew was standing around her now, listening to the mandatory safety talk. She was making sure everyone had their life jackets and all the necessary gear to travel safely down the river. Mia was a bit nervous about the time of year that they were taking this trip. It was April, and you could still see snow on the ridges of the Canyon. The air was a little chilly, but it warmed up as the sun peeked from behind the clouds.

Mia drifted away in her thoughts. She wanted to get into the mindset of rafting. The cold water impressed her. Suddenly she felt a presence. The regal man had stepped close to her, looking deep into her eyes while commenting about the sun. She could barely make out what he was saying. She felt entranced. Taken by surprise, Mia mumbled about how wonderful the warmth felt.

"Mia, we need your help," she heard somebody calling. The man stepped aside, and she went to help her friends. Ten minutes later, she finally looked up. "Where is he?" she thought. He was nowhere to be seen. Now, suddenly, Mia really wanted to talk to him. After looking everywhere, she went to the park ranger, who was still talking to the crew. "Where did your colleague go?" she interrupted the ranger. "Who?" "Your colleague." Mia repeated. "I came alone," the park ranger answered.

Mia was taken aback. What had just happened? She felt at a loss. She first asked her friends if they had seen him. Nobody had noticed him. "How could that be," she wondered. "He was hard to miss." Mia finally went to her husband, Mickey, who was still busy rigging their raft, and asked him, "Did you see the man who approached me earlier, regal-looking with a unique presence?"

"I did," Mickey said. "I even had a strange feeling. There was something about him that caught my eye, actually all my senses. It felt like a déjà vu, so familiar and at the same time so protective." Mia was relieved. She asked every crewmember again, but none of them had seen him. She was elated, though, that her husband had.

Mia sat down for a moment on a big rock, close to the river's edge, away from the group. She tried to reconnect with the energy. This time she felt dizzy, as if she were being pulled into a vortex, and she suddenly remembered her first trip to the Canyon. She could feel and see every detail of it, and she recalled not getting a good night's sleep.

The camp they had chosen for the night was a few miles above the infamous rapid called "Lava Falls," the one that had nearly made her renounce ever attempting a trip down the Colorado River in the Grand Canyon. Ever since she had heard people talking about it, this rapid had grown in size and might in Mia's mind.

They spent a good hour and a half tying everything down on the raft, just in case they flipped over. They didn't do that as a bad omen, just as a preventive measure. Previous groups who hadn't taken this precaution had lost everything in their boats when they flipped. The last step was to put a net over the whole cargo area. Relieved, they all looked at each other, ready to leave shore now and get over this first hurdle. Shortly before the rapid, they stopped to scout it. Depending on the water level, they would have to approach the rapid at different angles. Meanwhile, Mia was nearly nauseated at the thought of it. She could walk around the rapid instead, but she felt that she and Mickey were a team. They would go through it together.

The guys in the lead boat finished scouting. They headed back to their raft, ready to face the rapid. The rest of the crew would watch. They had a perfect run. As some say, a good run is over in twenty seconds. Mia and Mickey were second in line. Mia was at the bow of the raft, holding on. All was smooth – when suddenly a snake-like wave slithered up, out of the blue, and grabbed the front left side of the boat, lifting it straight up. Mia, with all her might, tried to counteract it. The wave destabilized Mickey's aim. It pushed them to the center of the rapid, where a sharp drop hungrily grabs any raft that passes too close. In slow motion, Mia saw the bow of the boat rise higher and higher. Desperately she held on, but the river current was strong. The raft just flipped over her. She couldn't see what was happening to Mickey. When she hit the water it was like a shock — it was only fifty degrees Fahrenheit.

Under the raft, Mia instantly searched for a way out. She knew to grope for the edge, where Mickey had added a safety line. Her hands hit a few undefined objects before she could grab the rope. She pulled herself out from under the boat. Waves battered her face. It was hard to see where she was, but at least she could breathe again. A few seconds went by, which seemed like an eternity. "By now, we certainly have run through the whole Lava Falls Rapid," she thought. "The Lower Lava Rapid must be right around the corner." Mia was just holding onto the raft and going with the flow, when another big wave pushed her back underneath it.

Suddenly she felt a rope around her neck. "Where did this one come from?" she thought. "Oh, no – the bowline must have come uncoiled!" Panicked, she tried to pull it off, but it got tighter. Just like in a movie, her life started to pass by in front of her eyes — all she had done and what she still planned to do.

Mia was gasping for air, when she started to see a light and hear a voice: "This is your time to choose. You can let go and do your work in another dimension, or you can finish your life's purpose on this plane. You will have to stand up for yourself, though. If you don't, your husband will sacrifice himself and leave this life so that you won't feel that you have to carry his burden, too. It is your choice. Know you are loved."

The voice and the light disappeared. Forcefully, Mia thought, "I don't have time to die." At that moment, the rope disappeared, and she was pushed out from under the raft to the surface of the water. Again, she groped around for the safety line and found it. Suddenly a shadow hovered over her. She looked up and saw another raft close by, and a hand being held out to her. "Let go of your boat," she heard. She was scared of letting go. She finally did, since the safe haven was so tempting. "Where is Mickey?" she asked, now holding onto the other raft. She was so tired. She didn't have the strength to climb into the raft by herself. Her friend grabbed her by her life jacket and pulled her in, to safety. "No worries; another crew picked him up," he said. "He is okay."

A shiver rippled through Mia. She took a deep breath. "Where did I go?" she thought, as she opened her eyes. Sitting on a rock, looking at the river, Mia again heard the same words she had heard earlier, and more: "I am glad you came back. We had to make sure you were doing this of your own volition. I am the Keeper of the Canyon, and there are many things I want to show you. Go and continue the trip you had planned to do. You will be safe. I have chosen you and your husband to gather all the information — past, present and future – to share with the world. You actually have come from the future. Just use all your senses, and tell and rewrite the history."

The energies of the apparition lingered for quite some time. Mia felt shaken, to every cell of her body. There was a sense of a bigger purpose, of some kind of anticipation she couldn't exactly pinpoint. She got up and walked over to Mickey. She told him the whole story. "It was the same energy signature I felt when that man only you and I saw approached me," Mia explained. Her husband also still felt the extraordinary energy of — as they now knew him to be — the Keeper of the Canyon.

They finished rigging their raft and put up their tent. The night was slowly approaching and the almost full moon was rising above the edge of the Canyon. The snow clouds had moved away.

Mia woke up, pulling the covers up to her chin. "Why do I feel cold? I must have dreamt once again," she thought, looking at the atomic clock. It had stopped.

She turned on her sound machine. It had a library of all kinds of nature sounds, such as birds, bees, thunder, rain, and wind. She loved to listen to bird songs, especially the ones before sunrise on a spring morning. It was like a meditation, a communion with nature. There was something so refreshing about it, and it helped her prepare for the day, peacefully.

Finally, she got up. She remembered that she had a guest waiting in the adjacent apartment. They had a lot of work to do.

Mia went into her antique kitchen, picked up her French press and boiled water. She opened the coffee can. A distinct aroma filled the air, rich and inviting. After grinding the coffee beans, she transferred the powder into the French press and poured the hot water over it. She loved the whole process. It was part of her morning salutation. Then she walked over to wake Michael.

"The most beautiful experience we can have is the mysterious. It is the fundamental emotion that stands at the cradle of true art and true science."
— Albert Einstein

Chapter Twelve

Memories of the Past

Michael had found it hard to go to sleep, even though the bed felt heavenly. Too many subjects had been triggered that day, and he and Mia hadn't had enough time to talk about them. He had to find out if he was having the same symptoms Mia had. "I guess I need to fall asleep, which will lead me to that portal Mia seems to go through every time. She hasn't mentioned a portal, but there must be a trigger point. I will have to count sheep."

His grandmother had told him about counting sheep when you can't sleep. He didn't really see the point, but he liked the little creatures. He could picture them hopping around. That made him smile, and he started to relax. One, two, three, four... ten...

twenty… thirty-three – and he was out. He perceived himself passing through a kind of portal. Michael's galactic body started to tremble and become itchy. It felt as though he was shedding his old skin, and replacing it with a new one.

He had just entered a huge, very high-tech lab. It was built into a mountain, protected from indiscreet eyes. This lab wasn't like anything he had ever seen before – and he had seen quite a few during his travels throughout the galaxies. Something made him feel uneasy. As he looked around, he felt a weird energy present. He could see some creatures that looked like a combination of human and animal.

It was an interesting experience for Michael. He knew he was part of this lab, but he also sensed that he was coming from another lifetime and galaxy. Mia hadn't talked about any of this. They would have to compare notes. He felt like a spying, hidden camera, but he tried to fit in, and he concentrated on what he was doing.

Suddenly someone looked over his shoulder, while he was making an adjustment to some kind of tool in front of him. "You are not doing what I asked you to do," he heard.

He could feel a warm, foul breath on his neck. "Remember, the continent Mu sank because of people like you. You are always looking for the good – instead of moving science forward with the help of these half-humans, who don't even remember what they are doing and why. We are in Atlantis. We are advanced in technology, and we don't have time to get into spirituality and such anymore. Those times have passed. You are here because we want to use your knowledge to create weapons."

Cold sweat was creeping all over Michael's body, like cellular memories coming back. He remembered working with an outstanding group of scientists, aiming for the highest good of all. They had been infiltrated, turned in and put under tight guard. A few power mongers had been able to destabilize a previously balanced society, and slowly but surely they took the command into their hands. The situation had worsened rapidly. With a few colleagues, Michael barely managed to escape from Atlantis, and they took their findings far away to a secure location. He had no idea what had happened to the remaining scientists, his friends. He just knew that the continent eventually sank into the ocean.

The stale breath of whoever was behind him disappeared. He didn't see who or what it was. He was sweating due to what he had just been told, but also from fires that were burning all around the lab. One of the half-human, half-animal creatures came over to Michael and sniffed him out. Michael dropped the tool he had in his hand. The sharp point hit his foot. He let out a scream.

Drenched in his own sweat, Michael woke up. "What the heck was that? This is abominable. Was that really Atlantis? Not the one I had imagined. I knew it had gotten bad toward the end, but that?!" He was horrified. He looked at the clock. It was already after 0800 hours. "How could that be? I am actually glad it is already morning. I need to get out of this space, and I need a shower. I feel dirty – right down to my bones." He alternated between cold and warm water, and rubbed himself down with a mixture of salt and soap. The water was held in a type of closed circuit, purifying itself once it hit the shower floor and immediately pumping back around, fresh as spring water. After ten minutes, Michael felt clean enough to step out of the shower and get dressed.

At that moment he heard a knock at the door, and Mia stepped in. All his anguish vanished. He felt relieved. "Oh, what a look. What happened? Did a comet hit you? Don't tell me you didn't like my down bed," Mia said in one breath.

"Oh, the bed was heavenly," Michael assured her. "But I had a horrible dream. Actually, I don't think it was a dream. I went through some type of portal, and found myself in an Atlantean laboratory before the continent sank. They had captured me to use my scientific knowledge for their own destructive power, whereas my team had planned to use it to prevent a disaster."

"Why would this type of past life come up now?" Mia wondered. Michael just shook his head in disbelief and disgust, and followed his train of thought. "We need to make a roadmap. What is each of us dreaming? Where are we — let's call it 'time- or soul-traveling' — and why? I think we will get some answers this way. Everything is linked."

"Now, at least, we know that you too are going back to other lifetimes," Mia commented, astonished to think that they had just met two days ago – which now seemed like an eternity. "We both need a good breakfast and strong coffee. After that, we can have a serious talk. For now, come over to my place. The coffee is already brewed."

A heavenly smell engulfed the whole kitchen. It felt like stepping into another, unique world, a "Land of Cockaigne," where food is plentiful. On the stove top were pots and pans full of delicious soup, scrambled eggs, sausage and hash browns; on the table were fresh bread, homemade jam, butter, cheese, yogurt and all sorts of fresh fruit. Michael had never seen such a bountiful breakfast table. "What a food fairy you are, Mia," he said, looking at her in awe. "Your archeological skills are broader than anybody's I've ever known. You certainly are keeping the past alive, even in your home. This is archeology of the senses in its living form," he admired.

Mia blushed a bit, and just smiled. They sat down to eat. In silence, they enjoyed every bite of food and each other's company. Michael couldn't remember the last time he'd had a homemade meal fresh from the stove and not from the replicator. Maybe it was when his grandmother made him a birthday cake? It felt like a morning meditation for his taste buds.

After they finished breakfast, Mia invited Michael to join her in the lab. "Let's gather all the information we both have," she suggested, "as we said earlier.

"I wanted to tell you that once again, I went to the Grand Canyon last night. I gather that it was the same lifetime, but maybe a different river trip. I had an encounter with the Keeper of the Grand Canyon. He appeared in the form of a good-looking man, very regal. He had a strong charisma, and it felt as though he came from nowhere and everywhere. Only my husband and I could perceive him then. He said he needed us to return and finish our work of understanding the immenseness of the Canyon. I felt both intimidated by him and attracted by the idea, but despite being conflicted, I realized I had to continue."

"The Grand Canyon it is, then," Michael said enthusiastically. "I am fine to *have* to go there. Too many people in our lives have seemingly been involved with the Grand Canyon in some way. Let's get to the bottom of this."

"Funny," Mia said, "The *bottom.*"

"Yeah, yeah," answered Michael, with a smile.

They walked down the hallway. They had gotten a late start. Everyone was in their labs already. "We worked the whole night going back in time, remember? That is worth something," Mia commented.

"Our sorrows and wounds are healed only when we touch them with compassion."
—*Buddha*

Chapter Thirteen

History Rewritten

In the lab, the Grand Canyon map was still lying on the desk. Mia and Michael moved it under a bright lamp and leaned over, studying it once more. "Okay," Michael said. "You blacked out when you read the topographical names of some of the Canyon's ridges and mountain formations. They all point to something; let's call it 'Egyptian.' Reading the newspaper article, we were both surprised that most of the artifacts were quoted as being Egyptian. Some relics were Tibetan, though. Deep in a cave inside the Canyon, they found chambers with mummies and tombs, as well as a Buddha statue. How did they even get there?"

Pensive, Mia looked at Michael. "Over the centuries, so many new discoveries have been made. Your dream about Atlantis points in the right direction," she said. "Egypt was a younger civilization than Atlantis, but very advanced culturally with its pyramids, medicine, and mummification practices. Where did this come from? To me, there is a definite connection between Atlantis and Egypt. There easily could be a cultural legacy of Atlantis in Egypt."

Michael agreed, and she continued, "A lot of people predicted what would happen to Atlantis. I found two books on the topic in my grandfather's library, one by Plato[7], in his Dialogues of Timaeus and Critias, and one about Edgar Cayce's[8] readings. Both placed Atlantis in the Atlantic Ocean, and both agreed that it went through several devastating floods before its final destruction, around 10,000 B.C.

Cayce talks about a far more technologically advanced civilization than what Plato described. Between the timeframe of 50,000 B.C. to 28,000 B.C., this civilization used giant crystals in subterranean tunnels. These provided the main source of power. They were also used to balance the ley lines of the Earth and maintain its stability. In addition, the crystals kept a balance among other planets in the Universe. The Atlanteans developed flying machines, and a sophisticated form of communication and transmission. Later on, Atlantis became far less technologically advanced than before."

Mia paused for a breath, and Michael took over, "At first, everyone was thriving and had a good life, until a few decided to use this technology for power and deceit. They started to conduct a lot of lab research on humans, in order to create a race that would serve as slaves for an elite few. They crossbred humans and animals. The abuse got out of hand. The negativity took over. Powerful tools were used that changed the climate. These also created earthquakes deep within the continent, destabilizing everything. With sounds, they were able to manipulate humans and animals at a subconscious level, first applying them to align the body's energy centers. This was an outstanding discovery that, when misused, turned into an unspoken torture machine.

"Sadly, this amount of power was too great, and many scientists could not refuse to work with it. Only a few were able to resist and move away into the mountains, but they could easily be tracked down. Some were able to gather their belongings and leave the continent, but the influence of Atlantis was far greater than just the continent itself. Places touched by the Atlantean civilization were also called Atlantis. It was important for the fugitives to get away from these areas as well. They knew that the stability of the continent was in jeopardy. In addition, all that misuse of personal power, and mishandling of crystals, contributed greatly to the demise of Atlantis."

Michael was running out of breath while he was talking. The enormity of the facts was hitting him. Everyone knew about the sunken continent of Atlantis, but among his peers, nobody had really studied the detailed sequence of events. Being out in space had steered their research on a more galactic level. One scientist had recently mentioned, at the archeological conference, that Earth was a major key to a better understanding of the Universe. It was actually a turning point for a lot of the scientists' projects. They had been reminded that on a larger scale, around 445,000 years ago, the Anunnaki from Nibiru colonized Earth to mine gold, in order to repair their home planet's atmosphere, since it was deteriorating and becoming hostile to life.[9]

Knowing that gold was to be found only on Earth, they first landed in Eridu, close to what is now the Persian Gulf. Later, they went to the southern part of Africa and started to mine there. They were masters in gene manipulation, and they eventually created a new species, a slave race that could do the work for them.

""Getting back to the point," Michael said, "We need to take all of this into account, to help us understand how those so-called Egyptian artifacts landed in the Grand Canyon. The Canyon is not only a star portal, but also a gateway to Inner Earth. The Native Americans would call it the Sipapu, or place of emergence. That is where their ancestors came to transition from the third to the fourth world. The People are led underground to be cared for during cataclysms occurring above ground. Interestingly, it happens that the Sipapu of Southwestern Indians, mainly the Hopi and Zuni, is close to the alleged location of the cave and underground city discovered by Kinkaid."[10]

Mia was listening to Michael, whose thoughts were jumping all over the place. "Stop right there," Mia interrupted him. "Let's backtrack, one step at a time. We will get to the Canyon later. Now, back to Atlantis. You mentioned that a lot of well-meaning scientists and people from Atlantis saw the disaster coming, and they managed to flee the continent before it sank."

"Yes," Michael said. "Some left in boats; some just beamed over to other places. They didn't want their knowledge to get lost. They decided to go in every direction on planet Earth, and spread their knowledge to as many places as they could. One of them was Egypt. They brought and shared their culture with its inhabitants."

Mia was pensive. "You know," she continued, "I have always had a fascination for architecture. I started to compare many different places on Earth, and I was astonished to find that especially with sacred architecture, such as temples, the architectural principles were the same. In my research, I looked into Vaastu Shastra, an ancient science of architecture and construction. These texts, found on the Indian subcontinent, describe principles of measurements, design, layout, spatial geometry and more. They are derived from the work of Mamuni Mayan, who was an architect, a scientist, and also an artist, who lived approximately 10,000 to 15,000 years ago on the Kumari continent, which is also known as Lemuria and South India.[11] I first thought he was from Atlantis, but he was actually from Lemuria, an ancient civilization that existed prior to and during the time of Atlantis. There certainly must have been some connection between the two continents. It is believed that Lemuria, also referred to as Mu, was both a highly evolved and very spiritual civilization."

"Where are you heading with this?" Michael interrupted. "We are still trying to figure out the whole fuss around Egypt."

"I am getting there, I am getting there," Mia replied. "Mayan wrote a treatise on building and architecture, still taught today, as well as a treatise on astronomy and much more. He also described flying machines.

"I read that at one point in history, many cultures based their architecture, art, astronomy, astrology, and other studies on Mayonic Science, as it is called. This would explain the similarities in the buildings of, for example, East India, Mexico, and Central and South America, to name just a few. This also demonstrates how even thousands of years ago, advanced cultures influenced each other – and you can find distinct elements in places nobody would have fathomed, such as the Grand Canyon cave."

When Mia stopped, Michael followed her train of thought: "What we are seeing is that a lot of advanced technology spread out from Atlantis, and even Lemuria, influencing different continents and countries all over the world. Therefore, what is often called 'Egyptian' is in essence mislabeled — right now, I am just referring to the Grand Canyon. Egyptians weren't there. I feel that a small group of Atlanteans made it into the Canyon. They must have decided that it would be the perfect place to hide part of their knowledge and technologies. The broad spectrum of rock formations, especially crystalline rock, allowed them to activate their machines."

"This is what the Keeper of the Canyon wanted us to figure out," Mia agreed. There are probably more reasons. Some can be on a global or universal level, or just for our own soul journey."

Mia and Michael were standing side by side, looking at each other. An energy bubble had formed around them, causing them to vibrate in unison. Neither had dared to touch the other's hand, yet.

A buzzer went off. The magic was gone. The sound was coming from Michael's bag, which he had thrown into a corner of the lab. Mumbling, he pulled the interstellar communicator out. Usually he had it fixed to his jumpsuit collar, so that he could have immediate connection with his crew, but he had put it away, not to be disturbed, while he was with Mia. One of his men, who was on call, had discovered a malfunction. Michael had to return to the ship. "I'm so sorry about this, but I do have to go. There is a lot to ponder about what we've just discussed. See if you can find some more clues. I shouldn't be too long. Hopefully I'll see you tonight." And off he went.

Mia stood there, lost in her thoughts. She had mixed feelings. There was so much new information that needed to be sorted out. Also, she really wanted to go back to her cave dream. She needed to gather more clues to connect the dots. Mia remembered the first conversation she'd had with Michael, when he said he wanted to help her figure out how to return to a precise point in time without the help of a tech device. Although she could time-travel in her dreams, she never knew what she would dream and where it would lead her. Beaming over using a teletransporter gave her the feeling that she was more of an observer. On the other hand, a dream would allow her to immerse herself completely, and forget where she was coming from. To her, this was a much more efficient way to have the true experience of what had happened in a specific lifetime. But what if she didn't want to access these past lives through her dreams? She had a vague memory of one experience, where a simple fragment of a rock would take her back in time. This gave her an idea.

In addition to the storage unit, the lab had its own fine collection of artifacts and rock specimens from all over the galaxies and planets, including Earth. Mia headed to a shelf that had tons of small samples of rocks from the Grand Canyon. She scanned the samples, and picked one of them up. "I am going to see if this will take me back to exactly the place I left when I woke up from my dream. I want to know how Mimi fares." It was a type of rock that she had seen around the cave. "It will be more precise than using some artifact that might not have been made on site," she thought.

Part of her lab was a meditation chamber, which she had turned into a beautiful and peaceful haven. All the high-tech material was hidden from view. Mia rested her head on the soft pillows, which would change colors depending on her mood. She could see that she needed to calm down. Her head was buzzing with all the findings she had discussed with Michael. Knowing the soothing effect it would have on her, she chose some soft music she called "Music of the Spheres," which had always accompanied her in critical life situations. Holding the little rock tightly in her left hand, she clearly felt herself reintegrating her 3D physical body, and going back to napping in the Grand Canyon, but not for long.

An unseen force woke Mimi. It made her get up, grab a bag with a water bottle and climb the steep canyon wall. She didn't even think of waking up her dad. Mimi was in a trance-like state, not feeling the blazing early afternoon sun or the loose rocks that were falling into the depths of the Canyon. Breathless and sweating, she arrived at the cave entrance. The two men who were guarding it nodded in her direction. She lit a torch, and disappeared into the cave entrance.

An earthy smell hit her nostrils. As always, the coolness inside was a pleasant surprise. Mimi ventured further into the cave. She finally entered the big room with hundreds of mummies, stood there for a moment, then rapidly moved back into the hallway. Away from all the main passageways ahead of her, she noticed a narrow fissure, angled to the right. It seemed to call to her. It didn't look as though anybody had been there recently. She squeezed herself through, and landed in a more natural-looking part of the mostly hand-hewn cave. She felt as if she were inside an immense geode. In the middle of the space stood some kind of an altar. A few tools were lying around. From a small, hidden alcove came a glow that seemed to intensify. She stepped closer.

What she saw looked like a crystal, the size of a large hand. It was sparkling and shining in the light of her torch. "It feels as if it is staring at me," she thought. "What do we have here," she wondered, more curious than scared. She redirected her light, and saw that the crystal was shaped like a skull. Now she could see holes in it: two eyes, two nostrils and a set of protruding teeth. She knelt down to take a closer look. Astonished, she could feel a calm energy engulf her, which relieved some of the pressure she had experienced from the heavy energy field in the main passageways. Mimi looked deep into the eyes of the skull. She sensed a masculine energy emanating from it. She suddenly felt dizzy, her head filling up with a deep sound. Every cell in her body was on alert.

Suddenly she heard, 'I am Voice of the Inner Earth.' I know that my shape and form might intrigue you, but deep within yourself you remember that we once worked together. My friends and I act as a team to help you connect to Earth spirit. You can consider me a key. A key can open a door. You came here because we need you to tell the world what happened. Deep, deep inside in this cave is a part of – let's call it the motor of Gaia. The Grand Canyon is a union of hundreds of thousands of energy fields. This area is gathering and re-shaping them, to send them through the tunnels that connect the other side of the globe with Inner Earth. All of this energy is needed to hold the planet Earth together. When the continents of Mu and Atlantis sank, there were side effects that almost nobody knows about. I brought you here so you could tell the world, and eventually the Galactic Federation of Light, the real facts. For you it is still 1909, but you will be able to pass this information down the line in other lifetimes. You will have many lifetimes, and many future trips to the Canyon in the same lifetime, so you will get the message. The Keeper of the Grand Canyon thanks you for that. Go with the flow – and listen to the messages. I will guide you. Just imagine my cute face."[12]

The pressure in Mimi's head dissipated. She was breathing better, and she smiled at the last remark. She was still looking at the skull that just seemed to have talked to her, and thought she saw "him" wink. Then, slowly, the glow disappeared. She felt the urge to go back to camp and share the experience with her father. Mimi got up, hesitated, and then did something she had never done – she picked up the skull and stuffed it into her bag, guided by a strong sense of doing the right thing, and walked back to the cave entrance. The guards told her that her father had come looking for her. He was in the chamber with the mummies. When she entered the room, Paul was standing there, shaking his head. "There is something wrong with this picture, but I am not getting through to the others about it. They so desire something that the world has never seen before, that they are losing their scientific approach. The director wants a new museum – and that's it. I feel that there is some grave information here, and we need to learn to read the signs. I'll go back to the other room, and try to talk him into taking more time to strategize."

Mimi was going to mention the skull, but she felt she needed to sort out what she had just witnessed. "It might have been my imagination, due to all the sun and heat I have been exposed to," Mimi thought. "I'll let you go, dad," she said. "I need to ponder what I just heard before sharing it with you. I think it confirms your suspicions. I will tell you about it later."

"I can't wait. See you at dinner," Paul said. He kissed her forehead, something he rarely did in this man's world. "I love you, Mimi, and I am so happy you are here with me. Thank you, dear." He gave her a big hug, and went on with his mission.

Mimi went back to the entrance and sat on a rock, enjoying the beautiful view. They were up so high that it looked as though the river was lazily tracking its path. She talked with the guards. They had a tough role, sitting in the sun the whole day, but they were doing their job.

"I need to get my backpack and my diary," she thought. She slowly started her descent, when she felt a small tremor below her feet. "That is weird," she thought. "Maybe I'm just hungry and insecure on my feet. I haven't eaten a lot today." She saw a flock of birds fly away. Something must have scared them.

Then she spotted a herd of mountain goats, jumping with great ease over the tiny edges of the sheer rock walls down to the river. There was suddenly a sense of panic in the air. The rumbling started all over again, this time much stronger. She could hear some very agitated voices, and she ran back to the cave. The guards outside looked deeply concerned. "We need to help them!" Mimi screamed, heading for the entrance of the cave. "No, it is too dangerous!" they insisted. "Save yourself."

"But what about all the people in there? What about my father...?!" Mimi continued to move towards the entrance. One of the guards grabbed her and pulled her further down the trail. She tried to free herself. "That's my dad in there. I have to save him." The guard had a hard time standing up to her. Mimi punched him and scratched his face — she was frantic. She put every bit of her willpower and strength into the task. Then she vaguely heard him plead, "Please, go back to the camp, and make sure everyone is safe down there. We will see what we can do here." She stalled in her movements. His eyes looked like her deceased husband's eyes, deep blue and kind, but she recognized panic in them. They stared at each other for what seemed to be an eternity. Then another rumble pulled them apart. "Get out of here!" he screamed. With a heavy heart, she agreed, and ran as fast as she could down the steep trail. Nothing seemed beautiful to her anymore. Wherever she looked, she felt danger. After she turned the corner toward the side canyon, where the camp was set up, she felt an even bigger rumble. Then she heard an explosion. Things went flying through the air, and she thought she recognized the red shirt of the guard who had just saved her life. She was horrified. What about her dad? She couldn't even fathom his fate. He had only wanted to convince the team to take their time and figure out the situation in the cave. He'd always had a great sense of perception — his intuition never failed him. He should have followed it today, but he wanted to assure the safety of all. Mimi tortured herself, until she remembered that there were still a few people left at camp. "Bob's ankle should be better by now," she thought.

Then she saw him limping along towards her. He was ashen. "Mimi, I am so glad you are safe. Where is your father?" She started to answer, but the grief took over and she broke down. He shyly put his arm around her shoulder, asking, "Do you know what happened?"

"No," she said. "It all took place so fast. Dad had a hunch that something out of the ordinary was going on, but nobody wanted to listen to him." Mimi felt exhausted. She should have mentioned the skull to her dad, and what it had told her. She sat down and cried her heart out.

"Know what is within your sight, and what is hidden from you will become clear. For there is nothing hidden that will not be revealed," Jesus said.
—*The Gospel of Thomas*

Chapter Fourteen

Little Rock Moving Mountains

The little rock sample rolled out of her hand. Mia was abruptly pulled out of her time travel. It had felt like a dream. Somebody was crying. "Where am I," she thought. "Who is crying?" Suddenly Mia realized that she was sobbing. "Why?" Then her "dream" from her time travel came back to her. "I lost my dad in the "dream." Where were we? Oh, no, in the Grand Canyon, again! It is everywhere. Every cell of my body is yearning for it, is screaming for it. I need to talk to Michael. This is getting out of hand." She realized that she was not at home in her bed, but at the lab. The rock was lying between the cushions, kind of looking at her, with a stern expression. "Strange feeling," she thought.

Mia went back to her condo. She needed a shower. It felt as if every single particle of debris flying through the air in her dream had stuck to her body. It seemed like an explosion – but it was something else. She couldn't put her finger on it. This time she strongly felt that it had another signature.

She took a shower, got dressed, and went over to Michael's quarters, to see if he had returned from his task. She rang the cowbells and entered. She felt such a sense of relief when she saw him, standing in the kitchen, though he was covered in dirt. It didn't look as if he'd had the best day either. "I am so glad you are back," Mia said. "We need to talk. The Grand Canyon is haunting me," she added, "and it looks as if it's haunting you, too."

"What happened?" Michael asked. Still in shock from her "dream," she continued.

"I went back to the cave in 1909, this time while holding a rock specimen from the Grand Canyon that was similar to the ones around the cave entrance. I found it in my own geological collection in the lab. I got the idea from a dream I had a while ago, and it seems to have worked. It transported me right back to the cave. It was getting weird and ominous out there. My dad wanted to take more time to ensure that everything was safe, but nobody would listen to him.

"There was some kind of crystalline skull that spoke to me in the cave, saying that you and I need to investigate important happenings down there. Then I had a short discussion with my dad. He was so kind and loving – he always was – but he didn't really show it very often. We planned to talk at camp, that night. On the way down the trail, I started to feel rumblings, and I ran back to the entrance…"

"Oh, no," Michael said.

"Yes, I did. The guard caught me and forced me to leave. I owe him my life." Mia started sobbing. "Then, I heard and felt a huge explosion. I looked up and saw the guard flying through the air."

"Oh, how awful!" Michael said.

"And my dad was pulverized. I can't bear it."

"Mia, Mia, stop it!" Michael started to shake her gently. "I know it is terrible, but remember, we are in the second half of the twenty-first century on a galactic ship. We are archaeologists. I'll give you that. But this happened more than 150 years ago."

"Oh, yes, thank you, Michael, but it was so real in my "dream." Mia took a few deep breaths and continued, "There is something we need to figure out. The keeper of the Grand Canyon wanted me – us – to come back to solve the mystery, and the crystal skull in the cave had something to share, too." She suddenly remembered having picked up the skull and stuffing it in her bag, something she would have never done as an ethical archeologist. Normally, every single artifact has to stay *in situ* - in the place it was found - until recorded, and analyzed, and kept for further study at a museum. She mentioned to Michael what she had done, thinking he might find fault with it – but she was astonished by his reaction.

"You might have saved something that could be the key to our mystery. We need to try to find it."

"Remember," Mia continued, "we talked about Atlantis. The skull mentioned its important influence in the Grand Canyon." They both took a deep breath.

"Right now, I feel so tired after this "dream," Mia sighed. "I could go to sleep. Let's have supper, and then go back to the lab. We may have to meditate for hours, but we need to know. I also don't think it is only the cave that will give us clues. The Grand Canyon is the history book of the Earth, the Universe, and the galaxies – and I remember being told that history, at least Earth's history, has to be rewritten."

After having a gargantuan dinner – with Michael doing most of the eating – they found the courage again to go back to the lab.

"It feels as though we have lived for an eternity. I need a vacation," Mia said.

"We'll do that," he replied, "after we find out what is going on. This traveling back and forth is really tiring."

Mia and Michael walked down the hallway, and they suddenly had the feeling that they didn't fit in anymore. Coming from 1909, they realized that clothing styles had changed drastically. Mia imagined all the inhabitants of the mothership dressed like this. She mentioned it to Michael, and they both giggled. Passersby gave them some amused, and some questioning looks. It took the pressure off them a bit. Michael, especially, seemed more relaxed.

Back in the lab, they felt they were in a safe cocoon where they could jump in time and space, sensing that there was a key to the madness.

"First of all," Michael began, "we need to find how we can intentionally go back to the cave, to straighten this out. When I went to Atlantis, I passed through a type of portal, and then, when I was there, it felt as if one part of me was involved in the story, and the other was watching. What about you, Mia?" he asked.

"No, I just dive into a past life, and live it with all my heart. It is difficult to go through this. I wish I could observe, too. Time traveling, even with the help of that little rock, still didn't give me the ability to observe. I guess we are just different," she replied. "If only we could find the skull again," she continued. "It feels as though he would have all kinds of answers. He insisted on being used like a key. Let's look for him out there, if we can."

"Good idea," Michael agreed. They made themselves comfortable on the pillows. "We are going to use meditation again to locate the portal I saw," Michael insisted, "and of course, we'll hold hands. When we see it, let's both willingly go through it. I will be the observer, while you jump into the precise lifetime. That will help me figure out what is triggering it. Also, I will make note if there is a difference in your physical body, and if you are bringing any aspect of your galactic body with you. It could be a melding from one into the other. It can't be considered a dematerialization process, the way it would using the teletransporter."

"Okay," Mia said, interrupting his thoughts. "I like to meditate with music. It kind of puts me in the zone. But this time, let's make sure we meditate with an aim. We are looking for that portal. Music first for a few minutes; then we can hold hands." They both looked at each other, mesmerized. "Stop it," Mia said sternly. "This is work. We can hold hands for work!"

"Okay, okay. I didn't say anything – calm down," Michael responded. Mia mumbled something, and gathered a few more pillows. The music had already started to have a soothing effect on both their minds and hearts. "Nice music," he commented. She just gazed at him. Sitting next to Mia, he looked at her and said, "May I ask for your hand?" She blushed. He saw her reaction and just smiled. She gave him her hand, willingly.

"When you are steadfast in your abstention of thoughts of harm directed toward yourself and others, all living creatures will cease to feel fear in your presence."
—*Patanjali*

Chapter Fifteen

Signature of the Past

The music gently rocked Mia and Michael into a trance-like state. Their hands were pulsating, as a small energy field started to build up around them, and then slowly moved around their bodies. Soon they were in a cocoon of light. They were as one. Then, at the exact same time, they saw the portal or gateway that Michael had gone through before. A diffused light shone through, and they heard a penetrating sound. They instinctively turned in its direction, then glided to the portal. Everything went so fast. They each had a foot outside the door, with the other still in Mia's meditation room. Michael could see that the front part of her body had changed shape — while the back, still inside the doorway, remained galactic. It was more of an energy signature than a visual perception. There was another feel to it. This glimpse lasted a fraction of a second – and then the galactic body vanished.

"Strange. 'Melding' is the closest word to describe it," Michael thought. Then he, too, walked through. Internally, he soon felt a separation, which seemed to tell him that the process was done. He looked at Mia. She was standing in front of some kind of primitive-looking tent, in a side canyon of the Grand Canyon. She hadn't observed any of what he saw. She was wearing big, bulky cotton pants, which looked more like a skirt, and a loose, white, buttoned shirt that was letting the wind blow through. "Smart, in a climate like this," he thought. He looked down at himself, and was a bit less enthusiastic about his own attire. "Oh, right, he remembered. "I work at the museum." Michael was wearing a suit and tie, as well as town shoes. He could already feel the sweat starting to pearl on his skin.

"Let's see what is going on," he thought. "It looks as though the explosion – or whatever it was – just happened." Michael was taking in the surroundings, and he detected an unusual energy that he had only felt and seen when he lived in Atlantis. Also, the manner in which everything had blown up into a thin powder could only have resulted from the Atlantean detonator. His time-travel dream had reactivated his memory, and he recalled having been part of a crew that analyzed explosions to build high-tech bridges. They needed a clean slate to do this. Most of the bridges were built in rugged, canyon-like areas, where it was difficult to haul away all the unnecessary material. The detonator would leave nothing behind. That meant that the device pulverized anything within a certain radius of the job site, or even just a strip of a certain area, clearing space for something new. It had also been used for other purposes such as building new town districts, replacing the old ones. There would be no rubble to remove – just a clean, workable space. It had allowed them to do amazing work, but sadly, as usual, the dark side had taken advantage and misused the new technology.

The other possibility he suspected was that the archeologists and other scientists might have entered a time warp. He started to figure out what had happened. In 1909, the energies of the human race were still in the lower third dimension. When they entered the cave, intuitive people felt a certain tension in the air. Their bodies instinctively told them to stay back. But for others, their greed, and their desire to become world renowned, had pushed them to pass an invisible gate – which would lead to their demise.

Michael wanted to share his findings with Mia, but it appeared that she couldn't see in the same way Michael could at this stage of their time traveling.

"Mia, can you hear me? It's Michael!"

"Why are you calling me Mia," she asked. "You know I am Mimi. Did the explosion make you forget?" She was not in the best mood, now that she was back in the same upsetting situation she had been in during her dream.

He grabbed her hand and said, "Mia, it's me, Michael. We came from a spaceship in the future. Remember?"

The touch did it. She snapped out of her state. "What was that?" she asked.

"I sort of pulled you out of your past life, so that we can figure out what happened in the cave," Michael said. "But it looks like we can't do a lot here. We have to go forward in time, when the energies settle down. There is too much havoc right now. Let's go."

"I don't understand," she said. I need to help my father."

"I am really sorry to tell you that your father either disappeared in a time warp and is somewhere in another dimension, or he was killed by the Atlantean detonator," Michael responded, gently. "Let's sit down. And give me your hand." She was too tired to resist. He could see the portal again, this time from the other side. He let Mia go first, and she instantly reintegrated her galactic body. He did the same.

They fell back onto the pillows in Mia's meditation room, still holding hands. Neither one of them wanted to let go this time. There seemed to be too much at stake. They stayed still for quite a while. "I feel like crying," Mia said.

"I understand," Michael replied.

"Did you see something I could not?" Mia asked.

"Yes, indeed, I did. You have the faculty just to dissolve from here and enter into another lifetime. I do, too, but I am aware of a type of portal we enter, and how we each lose our galactic body. It literally evaporates, or the two bodies meld into each other – which is good, most of the time, so nobody can track us. I can be the observer on the other side, while you just live your past life.

It looks as though we both had lives in Atlantis, which is why the Keeper of the Canyon asked that we travel back together. He wanted us to see that many things in the world, and many technologies, originated in Atlantis. Also, we have to be careful with them, as much has been tampered with already. Some may even still be stuck, up in the cave," Michael continued. We need to enter the lifetime when you had just taken the rafting trip down the Colorado River, where the energies are calmer, and the air clearer, after all the time that has passed. We can be anywhere we want in the Grand Canyon — even past the cave area. Any time frame after the explosion should work. Maybe we need to gather more information. But first, let's relax with the holodeck in the virtual-reality studio, then meditate again," Michael suggested.

"Wait," Mia said. "Let me get a fragment of a stone that came from the area of the cave. We have a new, ultra-sophisticated machine that should give us the precise radiation of the day when the explosion occurred.

"Excellent idea," Michael responded. They found a good-sized rock sample in the spacecraft's storage unit, the so-called "Warehouse" of geological and archeological artifacts. "The machine will do its job, while we take a well-deserved break."

"Let's go, wherever," Mia said. "I just need nature, water, greens, forest!"

"Okay, so it is," Michael agreed. They got up and walked down the hallway, then to a lower level of the huge mothership. It was like a city, larger than any left on Earth.

The "holodeck" entertainment center offered them many ways to relax. "The only nature program available at this time is, believe it or not, the one about the Elves Chasm — a desert oasis in the Grand Canyon," Michael commented. "Who would have thought that what we're seeing and feeling here is mere virtual reality? It feels like the real Elves Chasm – an enchanting, shaded grotto with a waterfall and an emerald colored pool surrounded by ferns, … and probably fairies, too."

"And here we are again," both said at the same time. They actually enjoyed just lying by the water, taking a nap and not saying anything. After two hours, they felt regenerated enough to go back to the lab.

The results of the rock analysis were ready. "Look at this," Mia commented. "It's something

Dominique Severina

that never has been seen. This is not an
energy known in the Grand Canyon, and it has
an out-of-the ordinary signature. If it were
Egyptian, we would have enough elements for
comparison. Even the few objects we found
from the sunken Atlantis are different. It seems
that at least two forces merged in the cave of
the Canyon, and formed a type of wormhole or
time warp that triggered something similar to
an explosion."

"Good call, Mia," Michael admired.

The energy in the meditation chamber had
changed. Whatever Mia and Michael had done
earlier had left a subdued feeling in the room.
Their connection seemed to have altered
something forever. It now felt more like a
regeneration chamber, adjusted to their
energy signatures.

This time they sat down and, without
hesitation, held each other's hands. Their
familiar aura formed around them again. They
stayed in this perfect energy, enjoying
themselves. "Let me know when you see the
portal," Mia said. "I will look for it as well." As
soon as she mentioned it, it appeared again.
This time Mia saw it, just faintly, but she
definitely felt the pull to go through. She

instinctively knew where it was — the Grand Canyon again.

Somehow, Mia and Michael barged into an evening party. She instantly recognized, and remembered, that day at Blacktail Canyon.

"… She could still feel the melody tugging at the freed edges of her memory."
—Michael David Lukas

Chapter Sixteen

Blacktail Canyon

The day had been long. They had taken their time at Elves Chasm, a fabulous side canyon with clear, flowing streams. There had been a lot of smaller rapids to go through on this part of the stretch. Depending on the difficulty of the rapid, the group would first scout and then run it. Today they hadn't needed to do this. It had been an exciting, beautiful day. Mia was looking forward to relaxing on solid ground. Suddenly, she remembered that it was her group's turn to prepare dinner for everyone. Why did this have to happen on the day they were camping at Blacktail Canyon? Mia had wanted to go there when she had first read about it, and she had made sure that the trip leader would choose it for an overnight.

Mia knew about the amazing geological phenomenon known as the "Great Unconformity," which was beautifully exposed in Blacktail Canyon. This is a surface in the rock record, or stratigraphy, that represents an extremely long time in which no rocks have been preserved. It could also mean that no rocks were formed during that time, or that they formed but then eroded away. So at this precise spot on Earth, there is no record of more than 1.2 billion years of Earth's geological history.[13] She wanted to see and feel it.

As the group had done every evening, they had to unload all the rafts, set up the kitchen and tents, and find a discreet place for the groover, their outdoor toilet. The cooks would choose the ideal spot for the kitchen. For this trip, they had decided to hire someone to organize the food. That meant they just had to pull out the "trip's cookbook," look up the date, and search for the planned supper's ingredients. Tonight's menu was "Doro Wat," Ethiopian chicken stew.

"Hmm, that sounds good," Mia thought. It was getting late, but the chicken needed to marinate for half an hour – enough time for some hors d'oeuvres. Everyone was famished. "Give us a minute," she told the group. "We will be right back to tend to your hungry stomachs." Most days, the group had been calling it quits sooner – to enjoy and explore the surroundings of the camp, or to hike, read, or sleep – but today everything had taken longer.

Michael had already found the perfect site to put up the tent. Mia changed into dry clothes, as she couldn't stand to wear her wet ones much longer. The sleeping bag was calling, and she had to gather all her willpower to resist its invitation. They made their way back to the kitchen. The tables had been set so that the cooks could see the river running, while they were preparing the meal. Most of the group was starting to relax. One of their friends came over to the kitchen with his guitar. He had a way of putting people at ease, while providing a musical note to the cooking. Soon a delicious aroma of spices tickled everyone's nostrils – and everyone's mouths started to water.

Dinner was a success. Luckily, another group offered to do the dishes. By the time Mia sat down, it was dark. The stars were twinkling. That evening, the Milky Way was stretching across the Canyon. Other days, depending on where they had camped, it was parallel to it, filling up the sometimes narrow slot of open sky above. Mia lifted her head and saw the sickle moon, in the shape of a flat bowl. And just above was the constellation of the Pleiades. She let out a little scream, which got lost in some laughter and music coming from her right. She stared at it, covered with goose bumps.

The reason she wanted to visit Blacktail Canyon in the first place was that she had read that it was considered to be a portal to the Pleiades. All her life she had been drawn to the Pleiades, but she didn't know why. There weren't many people with whom she could talk about that.

Sometimes she had a deep, inner feeling that time was not linear. She didn't know if she was coming from the past or from the future, or if she had always been here. In the last few months, Mia had done some research on how other planets, and stars, were related to Earth. One article was saying that the Pleiades and Earth were deeply connected, and that specific places worked like stargate portals.

She wasn't surprised to read that the Grand Canyon was one of them. The geological layers in the Canyon coming down the river have an effect of building up, energetically, higher and higher. As sensitive a person as Mia was, she could not help but perceive it over the days of rafting down the river. It was a crescendo of energies, a preparation to something out of the ordinary. "I wonder what else I will discover at the next river bend," Mia thought.

Michael interrupted her, saying, "Time for us to go to the tent. The day has been long. Good night to you all." Everyone mumbled their good nights, feeling relaxed and sleepy after the delicious dinner and the full day of activities. Mia and Michael got up and walked around the bend to their tent.

"We had quite a day," Michael commented. We deserve some rest. Let's not time-travel back to the ship. We have more work to do here. But now it is too dark to explore the canyon. I know you want to check out the portal."

Suddenly Mia realized that this time, she had come back as an observer. Now she was fully aware that she was Mia, he was Michael, they came from the future, and they were here on a mission. They both had done that river trip in the past – and they would now need to gather whatever information they could find in the present. They could use this trip as a springboard to get closer to the cave, but they needed to know about the Pleiadian influence as well. Everything was going hand in hand.

"You know, Michael," Mia said, "Before we came here this time around, we had planned to go check out the cave, again. Should we take a little trip before we go to bed? We are both tired, I know, but it still seems like a good idea. Nobody will notice our escapade. We are out of sight from the rest of the camp, and everyone seems pretty much done for the day. And as I mentioned before, this is the first time in my soul travels that I have entered as an observer. I'd like to take this opportunity."

"I am up for it if you are," Michael replied. He and Mia sat comfortably in front of the tent, under an amazingly starry sky. They reached for each other's hands, concentrating on the area around the cave entrance. This time, they were both able to see the portal and go through it, melding their galactic bodies with their physical ones. They landed where the group of archeologists had camped in 1909.

Mia and Michael could still feel the energy of the people who had been there, even though nearly 150 years had gone by. The shock had been so intense that the souls of the dead seemed to be lingering there, not knowing what had happened. Maybe they were still stuck in a time warp.

Mia remembered every bit of that lifetime, when she was Mimi: How she had walked up to the cave and helped Bob back to the camp, the discussion with her dad about her childhood and youth, talking about her Mom, her hike back to the cave, her encounter with the crystalline skull, her discussion with the guards — everything before the deadly detonation. It was still a deep-rooted cellular memory. Mia backtracked everything that had happened – and she suddenly remembered that she had hidden her little backpack with her diary in it. "I wonder if…" she thought.

"Let's walk up to the cave entrance," she suggested, and Michael agreed. It was as if her feet remembered the climb they had done nearly 150 years ago. The view was still amazing. There was a roughness and a beauty, at the same time, that was breathtaking. She found the little side canyon. Pointing to it, she said, "On our way back, I would like to stop there. I have something I need to do." Michael nodded. They continued their steep climb up. When they arrived at the cave entrance, whatever hole remained had been barricaded, shut tight. They both knew that nobody was allowed to go near the cave. It looked like there hadn't been too much traffic there in the last few years. Nobody had dared to come back.

Mia and Michael sat down to catch their breath for a bit, and review some thoughts. They tried to make out what had really occurred, based only on existing written material from the time of the accident. Later articles even denied the entire existence of the expedition itself, and all its findings, especially after the museum refuted that anything had ever happened in the Grand Canyon. It sounded as if the whole story had been fabricated. "It is hard to swallow that pill," Mia said, having felt all that anguish and pain within her own physical and emotional body. "It still permeates the whole area."

Michael got up and started to analyze the walls. He was intuitively checking to see if there were any hope of finding a second entrance. "If the Atlanteans had left anything here, wouldn't they have moved it to a safer place?"

Mia wondered, then asked, "What do you get? Any Atlanteans left?" She too started to tap into the ambient energy. There was silence at first; then they heard a long, yearning, engulfing sound, like howling. It made them both sit down again. At last they heard a voice.

"We are still here. This is a crucial point in the balance of Gaia. Our energy is here. Some of us went to live in Inner Earth. We finally made friends with the Agarthians there, and with many other groups that have opted for life inside Inner Earth.[14] We are peaceful, and we make sure that nothing from the outside can hurt us – and we keep it safe for the surface of the Earth. We feel responsible for what has happened, and we don't want it ever to happen again.

We are working with the Keeper of the Canyon. All of us together from the Inner Earth, the galaxies, and all the universes are here to protect Gaia, even if it sometimes appears as though it could explode once more. There is work being done, on a regular basis, with a few Earthlings who tap into our energies and actions. Bring more people down to the Canyon, so that they can learn through symbiosis. Thank you for helping us. We needed you to know of the energies still present in Gaia's womb."

For a while Mia and Michael just sat there, trying to comprehend the enormity of what had just transpired. Finally they both stretched, looked at each other, and got up. "Let's go to the little side canyon, just below," Mia said. "I need to show you something." She knew exactly where Mimi had hidden her backpack in 1909, and she was wondering if it would still be there. Getting closer, she could see the little alcove, intact. The fissure in its wall was the size she remembered. "It is a miracle that it was spared from the explosion," she thought. She put her hand into the gap. It was dark, and she couldn't see. She slid her hand a bit deeper. Suddenly she felt some fibers, and she delicately pulled on the two blue threads between her fingers. They were paler than she remembered, and much more fragile. She tried again. Slowly a bigger section came loose. It was the top part of her backpack. "Okay, let's try again, gently." This time she felt it give way, and the rest of the bag appeared – a bit worn, but intact.

"What is this?" Michael asked.

"It is one of the backpacks that Mimi, or I, was carrying in 1909. This alcove didn't allow even one drop of water to come in. It's stayed in pretty good condition, considering the time that has elapsed."

"What did you have in it?" he asked with curiosity.

"You won't believe it. My diary."

"Are you serious?" he asked.

"Oh, yes, more than serious," Mia responded. Her hands were shaking. Delicately she opened the backpack. She pulled the diary, with its faded red cover, out from the bottom. The paper looked old and shriveled. She carefully opened it up. The ink had leaked in some places, and faded at others. She would have to stabilize it back at the lab, she thought, suddenly very professional. Then she looked at the writing and felt a shock. It was very similar to the handwriting she now used. She had persevered in learning to write cursive script, because she liked the look of it, as well as the feel of writing longhand. It felt soothing, elegant and very personal. Rarely in the present galactic age did anybody know how to write longhand. That was unfortunate, since handwriting could tell a lot about a person.

Mia's attention returned to her old diary. "My name was Mimi, then," she whispered.

"I prefer Mia," replied Michael, who was peeking over her shoulder. "Oh, are you still writing longhand also? My grandfather insisted I do that myself," he mused, remembering the fond times he had spent with him. Then he continued, "You have beautiful handwriting. It looks strong, fluent, poetic, and sensual, all at the same time," he commented.

Mia started to giggle. "Sensual, right. I have never heard such a description when it comes to handwriting, but it sounds pretty good."

Michael looked deep into her eyes and asked, "Is there a right time to kiss a girl who one has become very fond of in such a short period of time?"

"Why don't you try?" Mia replied, coyly.

He moved closer and looked once more into her eyes. There was such a longing between them. His trembling lips touched hers, full and rosy, and they fell into a deep embrace, warmed by the sun sending its healing rays. They enjoyed their moment out of time in the Canyon.

Michael was daydreaming along. He had kissed her, and he could still feel her lips on his. At some point, they had held hands again and landed back in Blacktail Canyon. They were able to time travel within a time travel. He was eager to talk to Mia about that. They were so tired after the long day – and their emotional trip back to the cave – that when they returned, they each just slipped into their sleeping bags, under the celestial vault, and instantly fell asleep.

When Mia woke up, she slid right back into her full integration of the past life. She had no recollection of coming from a spaceship, or even of the romantic encounter from the previous night. Michael shook his head, and took on the role of observer for both of them. He was back to being Mickey, her husband.

Mia had gotten some water in her ear when she went swimming, and now it was hurting and stuffed up. When someone spoke, all she could hear were metallic-sounding, distant voices. She was in a strange space, which had an alien feel. And her mood was a bit sad. They also had to cook breakfast that morning, as well as plan lunch, pack up the gear, and rig the raft. She had really hoped to explore the canyon peacefully. After breakfast, with tears in her eyes, she returned to the tent. A friend of hers recognized her despair. Hearing Mia's lament, she sent her to go and investigate Blacktail Canyon by herself. "You did enough. Go, take all the time you need."

Mia started to jog along the river, then turned into the canyon. It was still dark in there. The sun had not embraced its walls yet. She slowed down her pace. The narrow canyon walls seemed to be giving her support, helping Mia gather herself. By the time she arrived at a little waterfall, her heartbeat had slowed down. She fell on her knees by the pool created by the waterfall. Suddenly she was drawn to splash some of the water on her face: her mouth, eyes and ears. "She who can see, sees, and she who can hear, hears," a voice said.

Mia felt the urge to get up and start singing a deep "Om," the all-encompassing sound. Her voice carried throughout the canyon. Her whole body was vibrating in unison. It felt like an amplifier. Suddenly another voice joined hers. She couldn't perceive where it was coming from. She continued. The new voice was getting louder and fuller. Mickey came around the bend. It felt like a divine appointment. Meanwhile, little rocks were falling off the canyon walls. The sounds were so strong. He grabbed her hand, and in doing that, he turned back to being Michael for Mia.

Riding the sound wave of the Om, Michael and Mia found their way back to her meditation chamber on the mothership. "How beautiful," they both said in awe. Then she remembered, and shared with Michael, how ancient cultures and esoteric teachings point out that the divine aspect of human form and consciousness came from the stars. It was said that the

Pleiadians provided the blueprint for human consciousness, also called the "Codes of Light," hidden in our DNA.[15]

"The earth has music for those who listen."
—George Santayana

Chapter Seventeen

The Tunnels of Time

Back in the lab's meditation chamber, Mia and Michael were sipping a cup of green tea, one of Mia's favorite drinks. Their latest time travel had gone very smoothly.

"Let's recap what has happened so far," Michael said. "At this stage, we know that the story about the Grand Canyon cave containing all the Egyptian artifacts is mainly based on Atlantean history. When the continent was near collapse, a group of scientists searched for a safe place to flee and protect some of their secrets and inventions. When the geologist G.E. Kinkaid discovered the remains and artifacts, he treated them the way one would have during a routine archeological excavation, not knowing that they were all linked to a still-active wormhole and passage. He didn't realize that there were tunnels not only leading to Inner Earth but also throughout

Gaia, stretching from the Grand Canyon to Tibet and all around the globe. "You are right," Mia replied. "I remember reading that one example supporting this is the fact that some Hopi and Tibetan words have the reverse meaning. The Hopi expression for 'day,' 'Nyma,' is the Tibetan word for 'night.' And 'Dawa' is the Hopi word for 'sun' and the Tibetan word for 'moon.'[16] The so-called 'explosion' eradicated a link to a part of who we are."

"There are still a lot of things to ponder and discover about the Atlanteans," Michael continued. "They had a worldwide influence. I would not have looked in the Grand Canyon in this lifetime, but thinking like an Atlantean, now it makes sense to me. The Keeper of the Canyon needed it to be confirmed. Thank you, Mia. I would not have gotten this far without your help."

"It is our combined effort that allows us to see the big picture," she replied, smiling. "Our discussions were very enlightening."

"I know you triggered a lot of issues by going into the Canyon," Michael continued. "Most of them indicate that we are part of something huge. The message from the Canyon is, 'Don't be fooled. This lifetime is just a fraction of who you are and what you have done in the many lifetimes you have had. It is up to you to share this with the world. Go and spread the knowledge.'" Michael looked astonished when he finished his sentence. "Those words seemed to have been put in my mouth. Where did they come from?" he wondered. Even my voice sounded different for a moment." Mia just shook her head. Michael continued, in his normal voice. "We used Gaia as an example. There are probably many more planets that could be examined under the magnifying glass. You and I are of terrestrial descent, so this is where we have been asked to direct our focus. But it is time now to integrate the universal and galactic aspects as well. We are the ones we have been waiting for. Let's use that opportunity."[17]

"There is one more thing we shouldn't forget," Mia added, "if you don't mind my recapping history a little longer. It helps me to see the big picture better." Michael nodded his head in agreement. "Atlantis met its demise because a minority of power-seekers took over and started to control others' lives. This took place at least 10,000 years ago. But remember what happened in the first quarter of the twenty-first century. The situation on planet Earth was not far from allowing another Atlantis scenario to happen again. The New World Order, a totalitarian world government, had taken the reins. It controlled everything from food supplies and healthcare to the financial world, issuing only one currency.

"There were numerous internment camps located all over the world for people who were fighting or protesting against the new global government. The biggest tragedy, though, was due to genetically modified organisms, which had gotten out of hand. Genetic material from living organisms was artificially manipulated in laboratories. Its heavy use worldwide contaminated fields all over the world, crops that weren't genetically engineered. Toxic herbicides caused grave health problems. So-called "super weeds" and "super bugs" started to show up, needing even more toxic poisons to eradicate them. It became a vicious cycle.

"Throughout the world the farmers' rights, and eventually everyone's rights, were violated. At first, the older generations seemed to fare relatively well, but newborn babies' systems couldn't handle it. Fewer and fewer children survived. The population aged and was never replaced. When people started to use nuclear devices in their fight for freedom, the Galactic Federation of Light finally stepped in. For the longest time they were told not to intervene, but too much was at stake for Gaia, as well as for Inner Earth and all the galaxies and universes. It was time to bring Earth to a higher vibration."

Pondering everything they had discovered, Mia and Michael were more content than ever, feeling that they had solved some part of the mystery. They might never know the whole story, but this much had been revealed to them because they had been part of those past lives.

"All the work we did in such a short time has brought us closer together," Michael said. "I cannot practice archeology simply based on facts and physical evidence anymore. We have to train our colleagues to perceive the portal and go through it themselves. It will add greatly to future discoveries – we can start a new trend. We need to make this our next conference topic: 'The Grand Canyon and Its Many Faces.' It is a fabulous field of study. What do you think?"

"I agree with you, wholeheartedly," Mia replied. She was looking forward to continuing her work with Michael.

Once again it was time for dinner. They walked down the hall to Mia's condo. It felt good to be back on the mothership. The living conditions in the Canyon were much more frugal. They each took a shower and changed into casual clothes. Mia looked stunning in her light blue flowing dress. Magically, once again, she put a lovely meal together. She was amazed by Michael's huge appetite. It seemed he was always hungry — "a bottomless pit," as she called him. He argued that it was because she was the best cook in the galaxy. The compliment made her smile.

At the kitchen table, Mia and Michael started to compare the many different lifetimes they had experienced to their lives in space. "We take everything for granted," she said. "From water to medicine, rejuvenation chambers and food replicators. Can you see me sitting around the campfire in 1909, telling everyone that in 150 years their lives would totally change? They would have called me a witch, and burned me at the stake – again."

"Oh, tell me," Michael said. "You really intrigue me. We have the whole evening ahead of us and we deserve a little break. We barely know each other, except that our energies seem to be very compatible. Let's take this evening to become more acquainted. How would you tell your story through the ages? What do you remember?"

Mia looked at Michael and laughed. "It will sound like a weird story, but knowing that we both had many incarnations on Earth and other planets, I will just jump right in and tell you about a few lives I remember best. They have made me who I am now. I can start with my lives on Earth, which as you know have been quite a few.

"Having most likely been an archeologist in many of my lifetimes, my memories have been revived by the work I am currently doing. As I mentioned before, I was accused of being a witch, and burned at the stake, many times. I knew a lot about nature, healing herbs, astrology, and astronomy. In every single instance, somebody presented a written official paper decreeing that I would be put to death for whatever I had done. Most of the time I had just saved a few people in the 'wrong' way, or I wasn't following the 'right' religious path, for example. Also, thousands and thousands of innocent people were killed during the Inquisition, and I was one of them.

"In the twentieth century, I know I had a lifetime in which I went to the Grand Canyon, and down the Colorado River, at least three times. It feels suddenly so clear to me. I guess I was getting prepared for what is happening now. I am even aware that in that lifetime I was reminded of other lifetimes. I had taken a class in massage, and we were learning different techniques. I remember that one of the teachers chose me to show how to do joint mobilization. He grasped one of my legs and started to move it around. Then he did the same with my arms. I didn't like it. It triggered something in me. I suddenly had a vision of myself as a man in Roman times. I couldn't believe it when I first realized that I had past lives in different genders. In that lifetime I was a slave, and I had been forced onto a huge ship that we had to row from Massilia – now the French town of Marseilles – all the way to Egypt. I can still feel the sting of the whip, and my big, swollen hands.

"They sent me back to Rome, having decided that I was strong enough to compete in the games at the Colosseum. This amphitheater was designed for the greater spectacles and shows, featuring gladiators and wild animals. They made me fight against wild animals, and also against other slaves. I continued to win for a long time. But when they decided my time was up, they chained four horses to my arms and legs, and made them pull me apart." Mia shivered at this cellular memory.

"Oh, Mia, that all sounds terrible," Michael exclaimed. "I hope you had some better past lives."

"Yes, Michael, I think I had some nice ones with you. Do you remember anything? We certainly must have taken some trips to the Grand Canyon together. We have too much familiarity with the area for that not to have happened," Mia pondered.

"Oh, thank you for saying that. It eases my heart. I feel very protective of you," Michael said with a smile.

Mia continued. "I think that on at least two of the trips, you were my husband."

"Great, I love that idea!" Michael blurted out. "Hmm, very discreet of me. Oh, come on, Mia, don't you see that I am falling in love with you?" Michael exclaimed. "I just haven't learned how to say it in a romantic way. I am always surrounded by these techies who have only science and machines in their heads and hearts. Yes, Mia, I love you so much. I am even afraid to touch you. Just the feel of our hands intertwined makes me melt away." He sat closer to her and put his arms around her shoulders.

For the first time in years, she leaned her head against a shoulder she could trust, and let out a sigh of relief. "Do you know how this makes me feel?" she asked.

"No, please tell me," he whispered, with loving eyes.

"I feel as though I'm not alone anymore. I feel understood, supported and loved. Thank you for this gift... and, yes, I love you too," Mia whispered. They savored the moment.

"Let's move to the living room where it is more comfortable," Mia said. They got up. He wrapped his arms around her, pulling her head towards his chest. She could hear his regular heart beat. A shiver shot through them both at the same moment. He gently cradled her face and kissed her softly. "I won't forget this kiss as I did in the Canyon in our last past life together. She blushed a little. They went to cuddle on the couch. Still eager to learn more about each other, they continued their conversation.

"What were you like as a child?" Michael asked. "Which childhood impacted you the most?"

"I think it would be my second one in the twentieth century, around the 1960's," Mia replied. "I had wonderful, understanding parents, and I loved to laugh and smile. Some people even called me 'Little Sunshine.' Early on, I didn't want to be fitted into a box. I was curious about many things, but I didn't want to join groups or organizations. To me, everything institutional was far too forced and unnatural, as well as controlling. I needed to come from my heart. Learning languages was something I appreciated. It allowed me to approach people more easily. It also felt like a sort of gymnastic of the spirit to change from one language to another – sometimes in the same sentence!

I would have loved then to know about the workings of a spaceship – all the technologies and such. Once, when I was a child, I had a dream after some Jehovah's Witnesses came to the door and told me that the end of the world was near. I remember looking at the date on the calendar to see when it would happen. I didn't talk to anybody about it. In my dream, I was standing inside a high-rise building, waiting for something to happen. A spaceship flew close to the kitchen window and rescued my family and me. Then I woke up. I might actually have been taken on a spaceship, at that time."

"Nice story. I like it," said Michael.

"What about you?" asked Mia.

"I too have a memory of a Roman lifetime," Michael answered. "I think I was an engineer and architect then, building bridges and sophisticated aqueducts in order to bring water into their cities and towns. I was well known at the time. The government of Rome was hoping I would build amphitheaters as well. I refused, because I knew they would use them for gladiator combats. Little did I know that you died in one of them." They both got pensive at the thought.

"Later in the Middle Ages, it feels as though I was involved with the Druids. I think I remember you there, too. You were one of the priestesses. We knew a lot about plants and healing. We did profound work together," said Michael pensively, "here on Mother Gaia and in the Galaxies. How did this conversation start again? Oh, yes, we were comparing today's technology to life in 1909. Nobody could fathom that we would have food replicators. Imagine telling someone, 'Once you have a recipe, the machine copies it and creates the food the way a 3D printer would. I have to say, though, it may look delicious, but I can still taste the difference. It doesn't have the same life force as real food. To me the secret ingredient is love, which no machine can provide. I really do appreciate your cooking with fresh food. I'm thankful that this is not a lost science. Down the line, I would like to have a vegetable garden and chickens on Terra Christa. I don't know about having coffee trees," Michael mused, "but we still know where to get our beans."

"You didn't tell me much about your family in this life," Mia said. "Only that your grandfather hit his head under your great-great-grandfather's desk."

"Good memory you have, Mia," Michael laughed, and then became serious. "My parents were exploring the Universe, and they traveled where nobody had ventured before, far in the southwest quadrant. They landed on this small planet to look for a rare rock formation. Their scanner detected an unusually high level of toxic gas emanating from a cave-like opening, so they put on protective masks. Sadly, they stayed too long and their spacecraft became contaminated. They had observed some condensation around their landing spot, which must have contained a type of acid. On their way back, some kind of corrosion they had never seen before appeared on the outside shield of their ship. My father tried to fix it, so they would make it back home safely, which they did, but the extended exposure killed him soon after their return. My mother, who was pregnant with me at the time, died in childbirth as a result of this incident. It was something that hadn't been seen for a long time on the mothership."

"Oh no, Michael. Not you, too," Mia exclaimed, shocked to hear that Michael had also lost his parents. She knew the deep pain that was connected to such a memory. Although Michael had told the story in a composed, matter-of-fact tone, she still could feel a deep hurt inside him.

Michael continued, "My grandfather took me under his wing. An avid archeologist, as well as an osteologist, he taught me everything I know today. Instead of telling me children's stories, he read and translated every bone's story to me. He showed me how this skill provides information to better understand humans and animals, and ancient cultures – and to help solve mysteries. It goes hand in hand with archeology and history. I know people call me "Bonehead" because of all that, but it really opened up my horizons."

When Michael mentioned his nickname, Mia blushed a little. She felt bad that she too had used it. In fact, she knew his nickname before she ever heard his real name. Michael smiled and said, "It's okay, since it really describes my skills." Then he continued his life story. "My dear grandmother made sure our stomachs were full and satisfied. She was skilled in many areas besides cooking. She seemed to know everything about history – the true history – and was also fluent in many languages. With the two of them I was in good hands.

I wish I had known my parents," he added. Mia knew exactly what he meant. Having listened to Michael's story, in some ways so similar to hers, it brought her even closer to him.

They both paused for a moment, then Mia added, "There is one thing I've often wondered. I have always had the feeling that I came from the future. Earth seems like the only place that has the linearity of time. It really bugged me. Then, in the Grand Canyon I found that past, present and future are one. This just makes me think that the Canyon is not of this Earth. It may be a kind of vortex. I think that is why I feel so comfortable there. It is closer to what I always had, wherever I came from."

Michael and Mia contemplated what they had just discussed, each extracting the different layers that their conversation had exposed. They both felt more confident in getting to know each other. Talking like this had given them a better idea of what each of their lives had been like.

Michael broke the silence, "To completely change the subject, I have to go back to my spacecraft tomorrow. My crew and I had planned to do a loop around the Sirius star system. Every so often we have to go check it out." Michael turned his head toward Mia. She was sitting there with an odd look in her eyes. "What's up?" he asked.

"Oh, that just reminded me of a dream I had in one of my past lives. Once I woke up saying the word 'Dogon.' The Dogon tribe, in Mali, West Africa, had detailed knowledge about Sirius B, a dwarf star that orbits Sirius, long before it was discovered in 1862 and photographed in the early 1970s. The Dogon guard a cave with wall paintings representing the Sirius star system. They seem to have known, well before science and technology were able to prove it, that it takes close to fifty years for the small star, now called Sirius B, to revolve around Sirius A.

"They also were aware that the planets of our solar system orbit the Sun, that Saturn has rings, and Jupiter has moons – facts that Westerners only discovered after Galileo invented the telescope."[18] Michael listened to Mia in awe.

"According to their oral traditions, their tribe was visited by an extraterrestrial mission, from the Sirius star system, thousands of years ago. These dolphin-like beings, known as the 'Nommo,' instructed the Dogon about cosmology, which is exactly how I saw it in my dream," Mia said excitedly. In both mythology and history, dolphins are often associated with Sirius," Mia continued.[19]

"This is something I will have to check out while I'm there. It amazes me how things just pop up. All I remember is that Sirius, known as the 'Dog Star,' is located in the constellation Canis Major. This brightest star in Earth's sky has been revered by many civilizations. To ancient Egyptians, it was the most important star of all, and the foundation of their entire religious system. Sirius was associated with the beginning of the annual Nile flood, upon which Egyptian agriculture depended."

Mia took a deep breath and asked, "A trip to Sirius will take you more than a few days. May I come with you?"

Michael looked at her with a serious face and answered, "If you can take off work, that would be great. I hesitated to ask you. Actually, you know what? I'll write a short expedition proposal and count you in. Thanks for asking," he said. "Anyway, that had been my initial idea of working together in an effort to advance the science – and our teamwork. It's a perfect opportunity." Michael seemed pleased.

"We can leave sometime later tomorrow," he continued. "That gives us one more night in our divine beds before we go back to work." They both looked at each other. Neither wanted to make the first move.

Mia spoke first. "What if we continue our discussion in my bedroom? Just being together and feeling each other's warmth would do me wonders."

"I agree wholeheartedly," Michael said, with the brightest smile she had ever seen.

"Pretty handsome man," she thought. Her heart started beating faster when they walked towards her bedroom.

"I saw your bed," he said. "It's huge." As soon as she opened the door, they ran to it like children, and they both jumped on it as if it were a trampoline. "I am exhausted," they both said at the same time. "Hopefully the portal won't appear tonight, but you never know. Maybe we will go and scout out the Sirius star system," Michael said.

"No, let's imagine having this precious time just to ourselves. We deserve it," Mia suggested.

"Fantastic idea," Michael agreed. They got under the covers, cuddled in each other's arms, and drifted away immediately, as if something had already been planned for them.

This time the dream hit both of them as soon as they fell asleep. They were propelled out into the galaxy. It had a different quality to it, and seemed that it was not even the same galaxy they knew. It felt as though they had gone much further back in time, when Earth wasn't even an inhabited planet. They had a hard time realizing where they were really heading. They were traveling at lightning speed, faster than in their crafts. They defied every possible obstacle. Before they knew it, they had landed on Sirius C.

"Why here?" Mia asked. She was aware that they had gone through the portal. It was the second time now that she had time-traveled as an observer. She didn't know if it had to do with the planet itself, or with how far everything was from normal. It felt good to be the observer. It gave her a bit more control. The atmosphere was kind of dark, and she couldn't make out her surroundings. She tried to remember again what she knew about the Dogon, and their knowledge of the Sirius star system. In the Dogon legends, the Nommos descended from the sky in a vessel accompanied by fire and thunder. The Nommos required an aquatic environment in which to live. After arriving, they created a reservoir of water. Then they opened the hatch, and half-human, half-dolphin-like creatures jumped into the water. Why would she be reminded of this – in her previous dream, and in the one just now – with Michael detailing his plan of visiting this star system? What was it that she needed to see? As in the Grand Canyon, there was an energy of alpha and omega, of beginning and end, of continuity. She heard a voice say, "Whatever comes up for you, the fact that you are aware of this star system makes it more alive. You were one of its creators. You don't have to go and see it physically, but you did have to be reminded of it. This star system plays a big part in the history of the Universe."

"Should you shield the canyons from the windstorms you would never see the true beauty of their carvings."
—*Elisabeth Kübler-Ross*

Chapter Eighteen

Carved in Stone

When Mia woke up, she realized that she was not alone in her bed. At first she was startled, then she remembered.

Michael was watching her waking up. "How did you sleep?" he asked.

"Oh, it felt so cozy and wonderful, she answered, blushing slightly at the sight of his well built, muscular bare chest. "I know we went to check on the Sirius star system. I was told that I had been one of its creators, and that I only needed to remember that. What did you get?"

"Actually, something similar. I feel that the dream allowed me to do exactly what I had planned to do. It was more of a reconnaissance mission," Michael answered. We can postpone it, but one of these days I would like you to travel to Sirius with me and my crew." He continued, "You know, Mia, when you have dreams and hunches about the Dogon, as well as the Popol Vuh, it is important to look into them," he insisted. "All are clues, which we might not acknowledge at first, but which later can become building blocks for a new, higher level of understanding. Also, your way of time traveling has made archeological studies even easier. It is a bit like scanning the scene before you are even there."

Michael continued, "You've reminded me of the Popol Vuh, the Quiché Mayan book of creation. It is their written account of the creation of the Universe, and the gods and demi-gods who occupied it. It is the story of how they created man, and it describes the ancestors of the Maya as they journey inside Earth through nine subterranean levels.[20]

"Could we stop talking for a moment?" Mia asked. "It is such a pleasure to have you here by my side."

Michael stopped his train of thought and looked at Mia. He took a deep breath. "Why am I still "in my head" when I have the most beautiful woman lying next to me?" he apologized. He took her in his arms, and they lay there together for quite some time. Their breaths were getting deeper and faster. He slowly unbuttoned her dress while she was pulling of his clothes and started to kiss her face, her shoulders, her breasts. She was just taking it all in. She had forgotten how good it felt – so soothing, so loving, so completely blissful. It awakened all her senses. He caressed and kissed her whole body, warming her slowly and arousing her gently. She was getting impatient. "Oh, please," she whispered. Slowly he entered her temple, and together they found nirvana.

Lying there, Mia asked, "Where were you when I needed you?" as she happily cuddled in his arms.

"I have always been here," Michael answered. "We have been together over many lifetimes, I realize now. And I'm starting to think that sometimes you were a man and I was a woman." She thought about it for a bit and agreed. "You are right. I have a similar gut feeling. It was about time we met again!" Once more, they got lost in another deep embrace.

"Do you think we've figured the Grand Canyon out yet?" Mia asked, playing with Michael's hand. Our grandfathers and great-grandfathers spent years studying and exploring it. Do you know how your great-grandfather died?"

"No," Michael answered. "Actually, nobody really wanted to tell me anything about his death. But now I am starting to wonder if he, too, was in the cave when it exploded. The fact that nobody ever wanted to talk about what happened there makes me a bit suspicious. It is possible that he was part of the group that disappeared. The museum never wanted the incident to be mentioned again. They wouldn't disclose the names of the participants – or even acknowledge that an expedition of that sort had taken place.

"When you were Mimi in 1909," Michael continued, "did you ever encounter somebody named Bruno Santi on the expedition to the cave?" That was my great-grandfather's name."

"Not that I know of," Mia replied. "But one group arrived later. We had set up tents for them so they could all rest before their climb to the cave. I was in bed when they arrived. In the morning, they had already left, just before sunrise," she explained. "My father said they were so eager to see what was going on up there."

"That sounds just like what my great-grandfather would do," Michael commented, excitedly. "He was an early riser. He didn't want to waste time sleeping. 'I will catch up on my sleep when I am dead,' he always said. I'm sorry you didn't get to meet him.

"My family received a report from the Flagstaff Police Department that he had been in an accident a few weeks earlier, and had disappeared down a ravine. No traces left. It was hard for the family to believe this story. My grandfather must have done a lot of research into the incident, but he never got anywhere. It is still a sore subject in my family. Nobody wants to talk about it. So I presume that my great-grandfather must have died in the cave. Now it sounds more like a cover-up. I don't know if anybody else looked into the deaths of the other participants, or what their families were told. I know my great-grandfather lived a fabulous life, full of discoveries. That truly was an interesting time to be an archeologist.

"Cover-ups have occurred all over the world, throughout the ages. For example, many huge skeletons have been found all over the world, some measuring ten feet or more, proving that giants actually did roam the Earth.[21] Obviously, it was easier to tell people that this never happened. Did you ever read Zecharia Sitchin's books, *The Earth Chronicles*?[22] He conducted very interesting research using Sumerian tablets, which he interpreted as history, as well as the Bible and archeological findings, to prove that there indeed were giants living on Earth. Even the Bible mentions this, in Genesis 6, and refers to them as the Nephilim.

"It really is crazy to think how humanity has been manipulated over the eons, and that it was only about fifty years ago when things changed. But I guess fifty years isn't much, when you compare it to the whole time span of our existence.

"People throughout the world could not continue telling lies. They were more than ready for ascension. The problem was that many were stuck in their own beliefs and wanted to impose them on everyone else – and punish those who would not accept their views."

"Interesting," Mia interrupted. "Some people just 'have a cigarette after sex,' and others change the world."

"Oh," said Michael, "I can't stop thinking about these things, but I want you to know, I so enjoy being with you. It is the greatest gift ever. My brain is usually in overdrive. It's probably due to the gypsy life I lead, and being responsible for a large crew. It's always been difficult for me to relax for very long."

Mia cuddled with him a little more. She loved sharing her bed with this wonderful man. She was starting to feel, in fact, that she could spend the rest of her life with him. She was still smiling when he launched into the next topic. They would have to do some yoga to calm his brilliant mind, she thought.

"What I really want to do," Michael picked up again, "is teach people how to look things up, trigger their interests, and then have them do the research themselves. Every turn we take opens up another mystery. It would behoove all of us to take matters into our own hands.

"We can't return to the ways of people simply accepting what is presented to them, without using their critical minds to question anything. A lot went haywire in the world because of that, and we have also seen it firsthand. No more lies – it is time for the truth to come out. We are all co-creators, and we all have responsibilities."

"Okay, okay, dear Michael, let's rest for another hour, then we can discuss if it is necessary to take a real trip to the Sirius star system."

They dozed off for another hour.

"What does the artist do? He draws connections. He ties the invisible threads between things. He dives into history, be it the history of mankind, the geological history of the Earth or the beginning and end of the manifest cosmos."
—Anselm Kiefer

Chapter Nineteen

Long-Lost Friends

Once again, Mia drifted away. She saw a little girl around five years old sitting in a sandbox, building castles. It felt so familiar. She could hear the thoughts and see the visions of the child. The girl was not alone. All her imaginary friends were with her. She seemed plunged into a deep conversation with them. The girl appeared to be an old soul. In her eyes, you could see the reflection of a rainbow — a rainbow not visible to this world. Her friends told her that one day she would be able to see them in this dimension. She would hear them calling to her.

Later that afternoon, a family moved into the neighborhood. Suddenly the sandbox became filled with a lot of new, visible friends. Mia realized that the little girl slowly stopped seeing her invisible ones.

The years passed. Once in a while, the girl would wake up, knowing that the dream she'd had was special. It always took her back to that one afternoon in the sandbox, when she was still a little girl. She remembered seeing round shapes, in different colors — red, blue, green, golden. Some of them had big eyes, small noses, pointy noses, big teeth, flat foreheads, sloping foreheads... She could still feel the excitement when they visited her. But what were they? Where did they come from? She tried to ask her neighborhood friends if they could see what she saw, but she mostly just got surprised looks. She stopped asking. One day, she felt lost, as if she didn't belong to this world anymore. She went to bed early and fell into a deep sleep. Suddenly, she saw a golden light coming closer and getting bigger – until she was looking into two deep and warm eyes. It felt as if she was coming home.

She heard a voice saying, I am 'Divine Being of the Golden Universe.' They call me 'Grandfather.' I bring forth the best in everyone. Although I look like a skull, I am much more. You and I have been together before, and I have traveled with you upon my wings, so it was destiny for us to be together again.

"Eons ago, you built temples for the skulls all over the galaxies. When you were young, the sandcastles you built were your memories of creating these temples. Your childhood friends were your students a long time ago, but they all have forgotten. I also have extraordinary healing abilities, and you can bring in my golden essence. And yes, we can go far together, traveling through all the galaxies and universes, wherever you want to go – and Michael is invited to join us.

"I am Grandfather, even though you played a part in my creation. Eons ago, I came to you in a dream. You sculpted me in your mind, with a great vision. The power of this thought helped create me – and here I am. I wanted to remind you of who you were – and now, we are a team together. Know in your heart that this is real. There are many more skulls like me, journeying here from all kinds of universes, ones where you and I have traveled together. Try to find me, and your little friend you saved from the cave. We are a lot closer than you think. We like to be called Crystalline Stellar Skulls."[23]

Startled, Mia woke up and grabbed Michael's arm. "Michael, I think I might have the solution to time traveling wherever and whenever we want to go. There is one condition, though. He said we have to find the skull that Mimi, or I, saved in 1909."

"Who said what?" Michael mumbled, emerging from his own dream world.

"I dreamt about a crystalline skull," Mia continued in the same breath. "This one was much bigger than the one I found in the cave, but they seem to know each other. He also said that his name is 'Grandfather,' and that they all are closer to us than we think," she repeated. "When he said that, I had a glimpse of this mothership. I distinctly saw the door of the 'Archeological Warehouse.' It's crazy."

She nearly fell off the bed as Michael jumped up. "Let's get dressed and go explore the 'Warehouse,' Michael nearly screamed. It is so huge. We never thought about looking there!" He was so excited that he even forgot to have breakfast. And Mia was too eager to find the skulls to even mention coffee.

"A stone is ingrained with geological and historical memories."
—Andy Goldsworthy

Chapter Twenty

The Treasures of the "Warehouse"

The "Warehouse" covered an entire level of the mothership. It was a living museum of sorts. First, Mia and Michael had to get past the hurdle of "Cerberus," as they called the guardian. He really seemed like the three-headed dog guarding the entrance to Hades. Though it was hard to evade his penetrating gaze, everyone on the ship knew the importance of keeping all these ancient treasures safe and in order. When they asked about the skulls, Cerberus kind of growled and said, "I wondered if anybody would ever ask. They are stored in the far end of the ship. Sometimes I see a glow coming from there, or I hear bizarre noises as if somebody is bumping into the walls. In the beginning I'd go and look, but I found nothing unusual. Now I think that they just come and go as they please. They are sentient beings, you know. I am talking too much, but I think getting to know them would benefit everyone. They certainly have stories to tell. They were of great help during the ascension process. We shouldn't forget that. You can take your time. There are many of them here, and I'm not sure where they came from."

Cerberus left them alone. He was familiar with Mia and Michael's archeological work, and seemed to know everything. They walked down the aisles. There were hundreds of crystalline skulls. How could they never have seen them? Mia got the chills, not from fear, but from recognition. It was like seeing old friends after a long trip. "It feels good to be home, again," she thought. She saw all the colored ones that she had perceived in her dream, with different shapes of eyes, noses, teeth, and foreheads; with and without glyphs or totems on top. She sensed the uniqueness of the Crystalline Stellar Skulls, sentient beings from different universes. Suddenly, she could remember and feel their reason for being – to bring healing, love, protection, teachings and messages from afar. She realized that they had been a big part of the process of opening up the world to other dimensions, and freeing it from eons of unwanted bonds, allowing the human bodies to adjust to the new crystalline energy. The skulls had helped the people on Earth prepare for ascension. It was only now that she realized the depth of this. They had supported and eased the shift from a third-dimensional, carbon-based body to a fifth-dimensional crystalline, or light body, and they did so with every living particle. They also had provided input to help smooth out people's reactions to what most referred to as "First Contact" – the supposed first meeting between humans and extraterrestrial life. As it happened, these meetings had been taking place since well before the Roswell incident on Earth, when in 1947 an unidentified flying object crashed on a ranch near Roswell, New Mexico. Some claimed it was a weather balloon, others an extraterrestrial spaceship – and that a body was found.[24]

Studying creation myths from diverse cultures often gives a hint of a probable encounter with extraterrestrial beings. The skulls had helped to clear a great many age-old, unwanted etheric implants from people. They had played a big role in settling peace on Earth, and ushering in the Golden Age.

Everybody was finally thriving, after having evolved into higher spiritual beings, moving out of 3D into 5D consciousness – and reconnecting with their galactic brothers and sisters. Love, forgiveness, compassion, abundance and truth for all had changed the surface of the Earth.

As Mia was thinking all this, she felt an immense pull to her right. She turned her head and not only saw "Voice of the Inner Earth," with his "cute face," as he had called it when they first met in the Grand Canyon cave in 1909, but also Grandfather, whom she had just seen in her dream. She couldn't believe it! Michael watched her change into a bright and happy being at the sight of these two skulls. She turned her gaze on Michael and said, "You didn't let me finish earlier. Grandfather said that we have been together before, and that I traveled with him upon his wings." Mia was getting more and more excited. "Michael, we have the perfect solution for our time traveling! From now on, we will ask the Crystalline Stellar Skulls, as they like to be called, to help us to journey wherever we want to go. Also, I think we can send them out on our behalf, while we remain on the ship. They can telepathically tell us what is going on and send us the necessary visions." Now they were both excited. They went to find Cerberus, and asked him if they could take the two skulls to the lab and work with them.

To their astonishment, he had no hesitation whatsoever. He just said, "I am glad they are finding a good home. They seem to be potent powerhouses, and keys to a lot of enigmas." They didn't have time to ask him any more questions. He simply vanished. "What was that?" they both wondered. Excited about their findings, they went back to the lab with their newfound old friends.

"Why are you trying so hard to fit in when you were born to stand out?"
—Ian Wallace

Chapter Twenty-One

Ride of Many Lifetimes

Back in the lab, Mia asked the skulls, "Tell us how we can best work together?"

Grandfather answered right away, "You two always seem so busy, so let's calm these spirits of yours. You know we are sentient, heart-centered beings! There is a technique you may use to connect with us. First, take a deep breath, put one hand on your heart, and get centered," he encouraged them. Mia peeked at Michael through her half-closed eyes. He already was getting antsy. "Cover our eyes with one hand and rub our heads with the other one. That gets us going." Then, with focused intention, love, light, and joy, send out a loud sound, such as 'PA,' and move your arms out and up to release this energy. Then rub our heads again, counting to three. This builds up the energy we want you

167

to send out. We call them beams. Sometimes we need lots of them to get to where we need to go. The movements and sounds give us the momentum for our travel together. You remain where you are in your physical bodies, but your light bodies come with us. Together we are galactic scouts. It can be great fun. We always stay invisible so the dark forces can't see us. We are able to keep you totally protected. Are you game?"

Before Mia and Michael knew it, they were flying over the Grand Canyon. It was like a movie appearing in front of their eyes. In a fraction of a second, they saw how the Grand Canyon came to be what it is today. The geological layers suddenly made total sense to them, even "The Great Unconformity." The whole history played out in front of them. Then instantly they were back in the lab, breathless from what they had just witnessed.

"Don't you think we're a great team?" they heard "Voice of the Inner Earth" ask. They turned around, and Mia thought she saw the skull winking at her, just as he had inside the cave in 1909. "You are the solution we were waiting for," Mia and Michael answered in unison. "You have truly opened our eyes to these new insights. Now we can time travel together whenever we want."

Mia could clearly feel the presence of the skulls in her lab, and became more focused. She had to continue her work analyzing certain artifacts that she had brought back from the Grand Canyon, which would give her more information for her ongoing research. For her own sake, at some point Mia would have to travel down the Colorado River with Michael and his crew to make sure they gathered all the data – a promise she'd indirectly made to the Keeper of the Canyon. She needed to feel the entire length of the river, not just bits and pieces.

"All is well," she thought. "This is a library that won't just vanish. It is written in stone." Mia laughed at her own joke.

Later that day, Mia suddenly remembered Mimi's diary and the few pages that looked as though they had been torn out of a diary and stuffed into her Grand Canyon book. They were signed "M." She had a hint that she might have written them in the twentieth century herself. The handwriting was so congruent with Mimi's, as well as with hers in the twenty-first century. "A bit spooky," Mia thought.

"You know," she said to Michael, who was once again studying the Grand Canyon map, "we never had a chance to read from Mimi's diary. We got a bit too busy that day," she whispered and smiled, remembering their first kiss in the Canyon. "I've stabilized the diary, so we can read it safely without damaging it. I also found some pages of a later diary that we need to look at."

"Oh, yes, the diary," Michael said.

"I know I wrote it, as Mimi, around 150 years ago, but it still feels like I am tapping into somebody else's book, into Mimi's private sphere," Mia continued. That is why I don't mind if you read it with me."

"I would love for you to read it aloud. I am curious to hear how Mimi – meaning you – felt about the Grand Canyon in 1909," Michael replied.

"Me, too," Mia answered. Her attention went back to her old diary.

Together they entered into the mystery of the Grand Canyon once again, which obviously was as much of a jewel then as it is now. They both were taken in by the poetry of it all. No other place puts one into such a deep space of peace, love and joy. Mia and Michael now understood the fascination and interest they had upon finding their grandfathers' and great-grandfathers' writings about the Canyon. It felt as if they were all connected, in time and space, with each other.

What an amazing feeling! They were planning to study their books and combine their feelings with the experiences they had just lived through… and they were going to do it together.

Mia was in awe. First of all, the diary was like a biography, but one about herself. Mimi was describing everything that was affecting her at the time. Mia could really feel how hard it was for her to live and work among all those men she didn't know. It was at the beginning of the twentieth century, when very few women worked on archeological excavations at all.

It amazed her again that her handwriting had barely changed. Reading it also revived Mia's feelings of the Grand Canyon, from the other trips she had taken in different lifetimes. To her, it felt as if it had all just happened. The two diaries went hand in hand.

Being in the Canyon reminded Mia that she was part of something much larger than herself. She realized she was connected to it in a profound way, and always had been. It is the "Source." It is a state of being. She was finding her way back to her true, authentic self. The Grand Canyon is a portal. She realized that even then, with only two strands of DNA, she had been able to tap into the Akashic Records, or "The Book of Life," which contained all the wisdom and information of the Universe, the galaxies, the dimensions. In that moment, Mia not only knew who she was and what she was in this lifetime, but also in eternity. It helped her recognize her calling throughout her existence. The rocks and stones of the Canyon, in a sense, invited her to define her own mythology. The Canyon's gift was to help her write the story of her lives. It was a path of transformation. Within the Canyon, she was able to find the matrix of all creation – as above, so below – the microcosm in the macrocosm – the infinite Universe. She was aware of tapping into the morphogenetic field, where every experience, every story of the universe is genetically recorded and available for anyone to access. Around every bend of the river, another story is at hand. And Mia heard the stories being whispered in her ears.

Going through her notes, she found in her precious, carefully saved diary and the few loose pages what she was looking for all along: the reasons why she had returned to the Grand Canyon, even after all the hardship she had encountered there over so many lifetimes. It touched her to the core to retrace the words she had written so long ago. "Listen to this, Michael," Mia said, taking him out of his own meditation, as she began to read what she had written in the twentieth century: "In the Grand Canyon, I feel like the seeker of the keys to the Earth, to the Universe. In its womb, I experience the web of existence, the universal source. I am part of the whole. I am one with it. The cosmic forces reveal themselves to me. I hear their whispers and feel their impulses. The Grand Canyon allows, if one can hear, to tap into a multidimensional memory.

"The Grand Canyon is a living library. It is up to us to access it. Every single stone, every rock, grain of sand, flower, insect, and drop of water, will release – to anyone who wants to listen – what knowledge has been stored within it.

"We are living in a time of veils lifting, worlds opening up and realities shifting. The Grand Canyon reminds us of cellular memories stored in our bodies. It allows us to access these energies.

"I realize that in some ways, I am searching for both my human ancestry and my stellar roots. It is a very strong feeling in the Canyon. All is pointing out that I can find an answer on this very Earth. The Grand Canyon is one of the keepers of the secrets. Lots of stories from eons ago concerning the Earth are buried and hidden away, but ready to reveal themselves. Listen to the riddles the Canyon has in store for you. Listen to the wind, the river, the earth and the sky. Only in true stillness can we hear, can the true wisdom be revealed."

Reading these lines left Mia once more enchanted, bewitched, and bemused. She also realized that sometimes with the journey, there are more questions than answers to be found, opening up the path to more adventures.

"That is what learning is. You suddenly understand something you've understood all your life, but in a new way."
—Doris Lessing

Notes

[1] http://in5d.com/recoding-to-12-strand-dna-sequence-and-entering-into-the-photon-belt/

[2] https://en.wikipedia.org/wiki/Where_no_man_has_gone_before

[3] http://www.nasa.gov/multimedia/imagegallery/image_feature_1249.html

[4] https://en.wikipedia.org/wiki/Maria_Montessori

[5] "The earliest Women's Day observance was held on February 28, 1909, in New York: it was organized by the Socialist Party of America in remembrance of the 1908 strike of the International Ladies Garment Workers Union."
https://en.wikipedia.org/wiki/International_Women%27s_Day

[6] http://www.spiritofmaat.com/archive/nov2/gazette.htm

[7] http://ancienthistory.about.com/od/lostcontinent/qt/072507
Atlantis.htm
The story of Atlantis comes to us from *Timaeus*, a Socratic
dialogue, written in about 360 B.C. by Plato.
http://www.bibliotecapleyades.net/stargate/stargate08.htm

[8] Edgar Evans Cayce: Edgar Cayce. On Atlantis, New York
1968 and
http://www.edgarcayce.org/_AncientMysteriesTemp/
platocayce.html
http://www.crystalinks.com/atlantistheories.html

[9] http://www.truthbeknown.com/anunnaki.htm
Zecharia Sitchin: The 12th Planet

[10] http://www.ourstrangeplanet.com/5-14-2012-expedition-to-
sipapu-the-place-of-emergence/

[11] https://arganesh3.wordpress.com/category/science-
2/mamuni-mayan-father-of-science/

[12] Information inspired by the Crystalline Stellar Skulls and
"Team Earth". For more information, go to stellarskulls.com

[13] http://www.thegreatstory.org/great-unconformity.html

[14] http://www.thenewearth.org/InnerEarth.html and
http://www.librarising.com/hollow/hollowarchives.html

[15] http://www.edgemagazine.net/2013/08/the-pleiades-
andean-mystery-teachings/

[16] Daniel Pinchbeck: 2012: The Return of Quetzalcoatl

[17] https://furgots.wordpress.com/2011/08/22/a-great-hopi-poem-the-ones-we-have-been-waiting-for/

[18] http://www.unmuseum.org/siriusb.htm

[19] http://www.darkwillowcreek.com/dolphinandwhale/Magazine/AncientKnowledge/Dogonandnommo.htm

[20] http://archaeology.about.com/od/mayaarchaeology/a/Popol-Vuh.htm and
http://www.criscenzo.com/jaguarsun/popolvuh.html

[21] pictures of giant skeletons:
https://www.youtube.com/watch?v=FC8wWsBKc88
https://www.youtube.com/watch?v=b_-vWCY5lN0 and
http://www.cultofweird.com/death/giant-skeletons-in-wisconsin/

[22] Zecharia Sitchin: The Earth Chronicles

[23] Inspired by the Crystalline Stellar Skulls and "Team Earth." For more information go to stellarskulls.com and read the book: *Crystalline Stellar Skulls. Who Are They Really?* By Terra Rae of "Team Earth."
Also go to gaia.com. You will find all kinds of interesting programs.

[24] http://www.roswellufomuseum.com/incident.html
https://www.youtube.com/watch?v=bl_8jQq1Dss

"The most beautiful things in the world cannot be seen or touched, they are felt with the heart."
—Antoine de Saint-Exupéry, The Little Prince

About the Author

Dominique Severina sees all humanity and herself as galactic beings and citizens of the Universe. Born and raised in Switzerland at the French and German border, she was an "archeologist of the soil," digging in the past to understand the present. From the mountains over the seas she came to New Mexico, the "Land of Enchantment," where she discovered the subtleties of the English language and its poetic, healing sounds. Now she is an "archeologist of the soul," surfing the present to understand the past and the future – doing healing work using energy work, sounds, words, colors, galactic energy to weave the precious thread of life.

Severina's intimate knowledge and vivid descriptions of the Grand Canyon are a result of multiple trips rafting the Colorado River. She has spent many hours hiking and exploring concealed secondary ravines along the route. An archeologist, caver, and healing arts practitioner, she has integrated her knowledge and research onto this tale.

Severina is currently writing a sequel to this book and also working on two children's books.